Pete Crawford.
As macho a cowboy as ever lived.

Sinfully handsome. And, like most cowboys, utterly resistant to settling down.

"Good morning, Pete," she said, keeping her voice cool. "May I help you?" She knew he would refuse, but she didn't want to be accused of being rude.

He looked over his shoulder as if he thought he was being followed. Then he faced her again. "Uh, yeah, you can," he replied, much to Kelly's surprise.

Her surprise turned to panic when he grabbed her by the shoulders, yanked her against him and planted a desperate kiss on her lips. A kiss that lost its desperation as it became passionate, warm, even hot. And completely distracting.

It had been several years since Kelly had been kissed, or even held by a man. She'd vowed never to let a man, in particular a cowboy, get close again. With that thought, she shoved her way out of his arms and slapped him...hard.

Dear Reader,

Brr... February's below-freezing temperatures call for a mug of hot chocolate, a fuzzy afghan and a heartwarming book from Silhouette Romance. Our books will heat you to the tips of your toes with the sizzling sexual tension that courses between our stubborn heroes and the determined heroines who ultimately melt their hardened hearts.

In Judy Christenberry's *Least Likely To Wed,* her sinfully sexy cowboy hero has his plans for lifelong bachelorhood foiled by the searing kisses of a spirited single mom. While in Sue Swift's *The Ranger & the Rescue,* an amnesiac cowboy stakes a claim on the heart of a flame-haired heroine—but will the fires of passion still burn when he regains his memory?

Tensions reach the boiling point in Raye Morgan's *She's Having My Baby!*—the final installment of the miniseries HAVING THE BOSS'S BABY—when our heroine discovers just who fathered her baby-to-be.... And tempers flare in Rebecca Russell's *Right Where He Belongs,* in which our handsome hero must choose between his cold plan for revenge and a woman's warm and tender love.

Then simmer down with the incredibly romantic heroes in Teresa Southwick's *What If We Fall In Love?* and Colleen Faulkner's *A Shocking Request.* You'll laugh, you'll cry, you'll fall in love all over again with these deeply touching stories about widowers who get a second chance at love.

So this February, come in from the cold and warm your heart and spirit with one of these temperature-raising books from Silhouette Romance. Don't forget the marshmallows!

Happy reading!

Mary-Theresa Hussey

Mary-Theresa Hussey
Senior Editor

Please address questions and book requests to:
Silhouette Reader Service
U.S.: 3010 Walden Ave., P.O. Box 1325, Buffalo, NY 14269
Canadian: P.O. Box 609, Fort Erie, Ont. L2A 5X3

Judy Christenberry

LEAST LIKELY TO WED

SILHOUETTE *Romance*®
Published by Silhouette Books
America's Publisher of Contemporary Romance

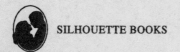 SILHOUETTE BOOKS

ISBN 0-373-19570-2

LEAST LIKELY TO WED

Copyright © 2002 by Judy Christenberry

This edition published by arrangement with Harlequin Books S.A.

® and TM are trademarks of Harlequin Books S.A., used under license.
Trademarks indicated with ® are registered in the United States Patent
and Trademark Office, the Canadian Trade Marks Office and in other
countries.

Visit Silhouette at www.eHarlequin.com

Printed in U.S.A.

Books by Judy Christenberry

Silhouette Romance

JUDY CHRISTENBERRY

has been writing romances for fifteen years because she loves happy endings as much as her readers do. She's also a bestselling author for Harlequin American Romance, but she has a long love of traditional romances and is delighted to tell a story that brings those elements to the reader. A former high school French teacher, Judy devotes her time to writing. She hopes readers have as much fun reading her stories as she does writing them. She spends her spare time reading, watching her favorite sports teams and keeping track of her two adult daughters.

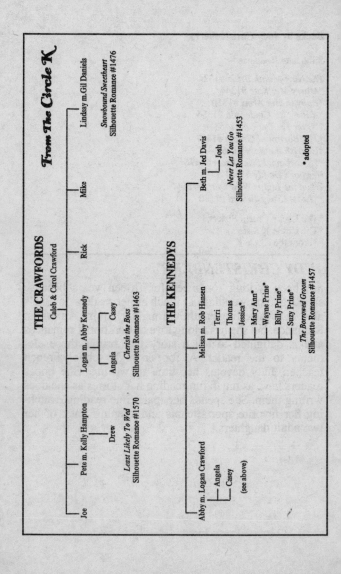

THE CRAWFORDS

From The Circle K

Caleb & Carol Crawford

Joe — Pete m. Kelly Hampton — Logan m. Abby Kennedy — Rick — Mike — Lindsay m. Gil Daniels

Pete m. Kelly Hampton
Drew
Least Likely To Wed
Silhouette Romance #1570

Logan m. Abby Kennedy
Angela
Casey
Cherish the Boss
Silhouette Romance #1463

Lindsay m. Gil Daniels
Snowbound Sweetheart
Silhouette Romance #1476

THE KENNEDYS

Abby m. Logan Crawford — Melissa m. Rob Hansen — Beth m. Jed Davis

Abby m. Logan Crawford
Angela
Casey
(see above)

Melissa m. Rob Hansen
Terri
Thomas
Jessica*
Mary Ann*
Wayne Prine*
Billy Prine*
Suzy Prine*
The Borrowed Groom
Silhouette Romance #1457

Beth m. Jed Davis
Josh
Never Let You Go
Silhouette Romance #1453

* adopted

Chapter One

Kelly Hampton looked up, a smile on her face when the bell over the door of Oklahoma Chic jangled. It had been a slow day and she was delighted to welcome a customer.

Her delight disappeared when she saw the customer. Pete Crawford. Lindsay's brother. As macho a cowboy as ever lived. Sinfully handsome. His broad shoulders, slim hips and cocky grin drew women like bears to honey. And, like most cowboys, utterly resistant to settling down.

"Good morning, Pete," she said, keeping her voice cool.

"Uh, hi, Kelly. Where's Lindsay?"

"She's not coming in until one o'clock." Lindsay lived on her husband's ranch outside of Lawton, OK, where their shop was located. Kelly hesitated but finally asked, "May I help you?" She knew he would refuse, but she didn't want to be accused of being rude. Just because she was allergic to cowboys.

He looked over his shoulder as if he thought he was being followed. Then he faced her again. "Uh, yeah, you can," he replied, much to Kelly's surprise.

Her surprise turned to panic when he grabbed her by the shoulders, yanked her against him and planted a desperate kiss on her lips.

A kiss that lost its desperation as it became passionate, warm, even hot. And completely distracting.

It had been several years since Kelly had been kissed, or even held by a man. Her dead husband, a cowboy too, had cheated on her. She'd vowed never to let a man, in particular a cowboy, get that close again. With that thought, she shoved her way out of his arms and slapped him…hard.

"Whoa!" he protested, grabbing her hand as she drew back to unload on him again. "What's wrong with you, woman?"

"What's wrong with *me?* What kind of store do you think this is? Get out of here before I have you arrested!"

"It was just a friendly kiss! No big deal. You don't have to get all upset."

"We've never been friends, Pete Crawford, so don't hand me that line. And this is a business, not a—a place where you attack women."

"Dammit, I didn't attack you!" he roared, obviously upset by her reaction. Again he looked over his shoulder.

He moved a step closer and urgently whispered, "Play along!"

She had no idea what he meant and would have demanded an explanation had the bell over the door not jangled again, hopefully indicating a real customer.

She pasted on a smile and walked around Pete. "Good morning," she greeted the young woman. "May I help you with anything?"

She and Lindsay, her partner, had enjoyed the praise they'd received for the up-to-date quality of their merchandise and the frequent repeat business they'd done. She didn't recognize this young lady.

The customer gave her a bored, superior stare before saying, "No, thank you. I don't see anything to tempt me...except maybe your other customer." By the time she'd finished, her voice had turned syrupy sweet. "Hi, lover."

It didn't take much brainpower on Kelly's part to figure out she was talking to Pete.

Pete's well-muscled arm suddenly draped itself over Kelly's shoulders. She jumped, but he held her in place with all that muscle. "Hi, Sheila. Have you met Kelly?"

Kelly had intended to protest his behavior, but the woman had insulted her merchandise. She waited to see what would happen.

"No, I haven't," Sheila said, and she didn't sound as if she wanted to.

Pete performed the introductions. "This is Sheila Hooten, a friend. Kelly Hampton, my sister's partner, and an old friend I'm getting to know a lot better.'' He squeezed Kelly's shoulders, pulling her a little closer.

"Kind of like a sister?" Sheila asked, staring at Kelly.

"Not hardly," Pete returned, grinning.

Kelly looked up to see him leer down at her as if she were one of those women on a pinup calendar.

"What are you up to, Pete?" she demanded. She didn't care what kind of game he was playing. She wasn't going to be treated like some bimbo.

"Nothing, darlin'. I just hadn't seen you the past twenty-four hours. I was starving for a look at you."

She opened her mouth to protest, and he kissed her again.

As she broke away, Sheila stomped out of the shop.

"Who was that poor woman?" she demanded. Whatever Pete had been doing, the object of it was Sheila Hooten.

"Poor woman?" he repeated, followed by a laugh with no humor in it. "She's more a—" he paused and stared at Kelly before he continued "—a witch than she is a 'poor woman.'"

"I don't care what she is. Just don't use me to play your little games ever again!" She turned her back on him and took refuge behind the counter located at the center of the side wall. "Now, if you'll excuse me, I have work to do."

Pete Crawford didn't like being ignored by anyone. He'd always thought of Kelly as his sister's scrawny playmate from the first grade. When he'd dashed into the store to plead for his sister's help, he'd found only Kelly. And suddenly he realized she was all grown up.

Why hadn't he noticed it before? But the only time he'd seen her in the past ten years had been at Lindsay's wedding and all his attention had been focused on his sister.

The instantaneous recognition that Kelly was the solution to his problem hadn't allowed too much preparation time. And Kelly hadn't cooperated very well. Fortunately Sheila had gone by the front window while he was kissing Kelly and returned to confront him after the slapped-cheek incident.

"Fine!" he exclaimed in response to her withdrawal, still standing in the middle of the store where Kelly had left him. "I'm driving out to Gil's place to talk to Lindsay!"

"Fine," she returned coldly, not bothering to look up.

He stalked out of the store, wanting to show his displeasure, but he had a lowering feeling she didn't even notice, much less care.

All the way to his brother-in-law's ranch, he muttered to himself about Kelly's lack of cooperation, alternated with thoughts of the slap…and the kiss. He didn't want to think about the kiss, but it had been something special. That old chestnut about kissing a lot of frogs before finding a prince—or princess—flashed through his brain, but he dismissed it. After all, he wasn't looking for a princess. At least not permanently.

When he arrived at Lindsay's house, he found her and her husband, Gil Daniels, along with Rafe Hernandez,

Gil's manager and best friend, sitting down to lunch. He was immediately invited to join them.

"Don't mind if I do," he agreed with a grin. He seldom turned down food. "I need to talk to you," he said, staring at Lindsay. "I can kill two birds with one stone."

"Gee," Lindsay said, sarcasm in her voice, "I love being called a bird."

"You know what I mean. Too bad your partner doesn't," he muttered as he constructed a Dagwood sandwich.

Lindsay stared at him. "What does Kelly have to do with your problem?"

"I, uh, well, I needed her to help to make Sheila believe—well, she wouldn't cooperate." He knew how protective Lindsay was of her friend and partner. Suddenly he decided honesty wasn't the best policy on this particular occasion.

Lindsay stared at him, clearly still curious about his meaning.

Gil, who had become a good friend since he'd married Lindsay, said, "Maybe you should tell Lindsay your problem first, Pete."

"Uh, yeah. I've gone out with Sheila Hooten a few times," he began. Then he held up a hand, anticipating Lindsay's response. "I know you told me she was bad news, but we had fun. And I made it clear that's all I wanted. But she started pressing me."

"For what?" Rafe asked.

"Man, you don't know nothing about women," Pete announced. "She wanted me to marry her!"

"I never said I understood women," Rafe said, glaring at Pete. "I'm a bachelor."

"So am I, and hoping to stay that way."

"Come on, Pete," Gil said with a grin. "Marriage is great." He smiled at his wife and reached out to touch her. Pete had noticed that Gil constantly touched Lindsay.

"You're still a newlywed, Gil. How would you know? Most women don't start bossing you around until after the first year, usually just after you've had a kid and know you can't leave."

Gil laughed, but Lindsay protested and her cheeks turned red.

"Sorry, sis. I'm sure that won't happen to you, but you remember Brad at Christmastime?" he asked, naming Gil's brother-in-law. "Cathy had him tied in knots, leading him around by the nose. It was pitiful. All because she was pregnant."

Rafe leaned toward him. "Eat your sandwich, boy. You're not scoring any points with either Gil or Lindsay."

After checking their expressions, Pete decided Rafe's advice was sound and bit off a big bite of his sandwich.

As he chewed determinedly, Gil sighed, then spoke. "If you made your intentions clear, then what's the problem?"

Lindsay gave her husband a disgusted look. "None of you know anything about women. Really, Gil, no woman would believe his warning. It's like waving a red flag in front of a bull and expecting him to ignore it. That's ridiculous!''

"Hey, I was trying to be honest!" Pete swore, his voice rising.

"So stop seeing her," Gil suggested.

"I haven't asked her out for a couple of weeks, but she keeps showing up wherever I go. And she hangs all over me." Pete sent a disgusted look in his sister's direction. "What can I do?"

Lindsay sighed. "Well, you could pay attention to another lady, but then you'd end up with her expecting marriage. Though why these women think you'd be good marriage material, I'll never know. You need a woman who feels the same way you do about mar—" She broke off midword, staring into space.

Pete glowered at her. "There isn't a woman alive who doesn't want to catch a man," Pete muttered. Gil reluctantly nodded in agreement.

"You're wrong. I know a lady who feels that way."

Pete looked doubtful. "Are you sure?"

"Yes. Kelly. She won't even consider marriage. All we have to do is talk her into helping."

Pete remembered Kelly's attitude when he'd involved her earlier. "Uh, Lindsay, I don't think that's going to work."

When Lindsay arrived at the store at one o'clock, Kelly didn't mention her problem with Pete. She figured the least said, the soonest mended. She felt sure she'd gotten her point across to Pete Crawford. She didn't think he'd try that "stuff" again.

Which was good because the "stuff" was bothersome. She couldn't get that kiss—those kisses to be technically correct—out of her head. But she would. She was determined.

"I'm going upstairs to have lunch with Mom and Drew," she said. "If you need help, just call."

When they'd agreed to be partners, Lindsay had no intention of marrying. She'd returned home after a year in Chicago. She'd bought the entire building and converted the second floor above the shop into a roomy three-bedroom apartment she intended to share with Kelly and Kelly's son, Drew. But by then, Gil, who'd met Kelly in Chicago, had convinced her to marry him.

Lindsay had moved to Gil's ranch. She'd offered Kelly the apartment at a ridiculously low rate, and Kelly had convinced her mother to move in with her and give up her waitressing jobs to take care of her grandson, sometimes also helping out in the store.

"I'll come down again when Drew takes his nap," Kelly added, hurrying away before Lindsay could say anything.

When Kelly entered the apartment, she heard her two-year-old son chattering to his grandmother. He didn't always get the words right, but he was happy. And she adored him.

"Hey, little guy, how are you?" she asked as she moved into the kitchen.

He beamed at her and held out his arms. "Mama!"

Kelly gave him a hug but didn't take him out of his high chair. Her mother was filling a plate for him full of chopped-up bites of hamburger, mashed potatoes and steamed broccoli. Kelly wanted him to eat properly. "Mmm, mmm, good. Look at what Grandma has fixed for you."

Mary Wildenthal grinned at her daughter. "I hope your enthusiasm works."

"Maybe if we bribe him with cookies," Kelly returned.

Drew squealed in excitement. "Cookie!" It was one of his favorite words.

"Oops," Kelly acknowledged her mistake. "After you eat your lunch."

"You'd better eat your lunch, too. I heard the high school was letting out early for parent conferences. I bet you're busy this afternoon."

"I hope so," Kelly said, sitting down at the table. She felt spoiled letting her mother serve her, but Mary insisted. After holding down two waitressing jobs for twenty-five years, she said she felt lazy.

Kelly followed her mother's advice. It meant her mother wouldn't expect conversation, and Kelly was afraid she might let slip her difficulty with Pete. Like Lindsay, her mother thought Kelly should date.

Kelly thought the one dating should be Mary. She was only forty-one, having had Kelly when she was sixteen. Kelly's father ran away to avoid responsibility and Mary's strict parents had kicked Mary out of the house.

"Kelly?" Lindsay's voice sounded on the intercom

between the apartment and the dress shop. "We're filling up."

Kelly punched the button to respond. "I'll be right down." She'd barely eaten half of her lunch, and she wasn't scheduled to work the afternoon, but a new business needed flexibility. After six months of operation their efforts were really beginning to pay off.

"But you haven't finished your meal," Mary protested.

"I know, but we need the customers. Come down after Drew goes to sleep," she added. They'd gotten a baby monitor so as long as Drew couldn't get out of his bed, they were okay. But Kelly was getting worried about his prowess these days.

"Okay," Mary agreed.

When Kelly got downstairs, she discovered they were having a run on the prom gowns. She and Lindsay had spent more than they'd intended because they'd found a new supplier with great designs when they'd come to market in Dallas. Today, it looked like their investment was paying off.

When Mary came down, she took over the counter, ringing up customers, leaving Kelly and Lindsay to the actual selling.

The store closed officially at 6:00 p.m., but it was almost six-thirty when Lindsay locked the door behind the last customer. Since Mary had gone back upstairs a couple of hours ago to care for Drew, Lindsay and Kelly were on their own.

"We did over three thousand in sales today," Kelly

exclaimed from behind the counter tallying sales. "I bet we're even busier on Saturday. We're getting a lot of good word of mouth."

Lindsay agreed. "Those gowns you found at market are almost gone. I think we should call the supplier in the morning and have them overnight some more. Today's Wednesday. We could have them on the racks Saturday."

Kelly beamed at her partner. "Brilliant idea! I'll call first thing in the morning. And I'm calling Addie McCracken. She wanted that plum dress and it was too small. I can order a bigger size if she wants it."

"Great! You have such a memory. I'd forgotten about Addie." Lindsay paused and then added, "With that great memory of yours, it's amazing that you forgot to mention Pete's visit today."

Kelly froze. That was a subject she had hoped to avoid. She attempted a casual shrug. "What's to mention? He was looking for you, and I told him where to find you. I hope that was okay?"

"Of course it was okay. So he didn't upset you?"

Kelly noted how closely Lindsay was watching her. "No, of course not."

Lindsay heaved a big sigh. "Oh, good, 'cause he needs your help."

Kelly drew a deep breath. "I don't think I'd be very good as a cowboy. Sorry."

"That's okay, 'cause he doesn't need you to round up cows. He needs you to go to the movies with him."

Lindsay smiled at her as if she'd already agreed to help Pete.

"Oh, come on, Lindsay. Pete can get a date in a minute's time. You know how popular he is. The women in town just flock to him." She was not going to the movies with Pete. Of that she was sure.

"You're right," Lindsay agreed.

Kelly released a deep sigh. "Of course I am."

"But none of them have what you have," Lindsay added.

"What's that?" Kelly asked sharply.

"You don't want to get married," she replied, her grin triumphant.

Kelly had told her friend her feelings too many times to argue with her now. "True, but I'm not going out with him. He's not going to use me to break some woman's heart. He can do that by himself."

"I know you'll find this hard to believe, but he can't. He warned Sheila he just wanted fun, no commitment, but she considered his words a challenge."

"Of course," Kelly replied matter-of-factly, understanding at once what Lindsay had had to explain to the men.

"Well, she's been bragging about how she plans to trap him. If he doesn't marry her, it will harm his reputation. If he does marry her, he'll be miserable the rest of his life. The answer is to start dating a woman who doesn't want marriage. You."

"I don't date." Kelly didn't bother to protest Lindsay's plan. Her determined tone, she thought, would do the trick. After all, Lindsay knew her history. She understood why Kelly wanted nothing to do with a man.

"It wouldn't really be a date," Lindsay said. "Mostly you'd just appear in public with him. The rest of the time, you'd be watching a movie you've been wanting to see—and Pete would have to pay! Wouldn't that be great? It'd only be a few times. And our entire family would be grateful." Lindsay shuddered. "Imagine having Sheila as part of your family. How awful!"

"I don't even know her!" Kelly exclaimed. "Do you want to come have a soda before you go home?"

"Great, but before we go upstairs, will you please help Pete—and me—out?"

Kelly glared at her best friend in the world, angry with her that she was backing Kelly into a corner. How could she refuse? Because of Lindsay, her shop was flourishing, and she and Drew no longer lived in the small trailer home. Her mother was with her and enjoying life, finally. All because of Lindsay.

But she just couldn't say yes.

"Lindsay, I just can't. I—it's—"

Lindsay moved closer to Kelly. "I figured, so I worked out some incentive."

"Lindsay—" Kelly began to protest, but Lindsay stopped her.

"It's only fair. And it's something you'll love because it helps your mother, too."

For the first time, Lindsay really had Kelly's attention. "What are you talking about? How could Pete do something that would help my mother?"

Lindsay smiled. "Well, I thought you might refuse, so I decided you'd be more agreeable if the two of you weren't alone. So I suggested you double-date."

"It would certainly make it easier, but I don't see how that would help my mother."

Lindsay said nothing.

Kelly stared at her. "Well?"

"The other couple would be Mary…and Rafe."

"Mother and Rafe?"

"You said you wanted her to date, to have fun. And remember those shy looks between them, when you both came to the ranch for dinner? I thought they would be perfect together. I suggested it to Rafe, without mentioning that I thought he was interested in Mary. It was so cute, Kelly. He ducked his head and said he guessed he could help Pete out, if Mary wouldn't object." Lindsay chuckled, pleasure on her face.

Kelly closed her eyes and swallowed.

Looks like she was wrong.

She was going to the movies with Pete Crawford.

Chapter Two

On Friday night Kelly studied herself in the mirror. She
hadn't gone out in the evening since before Drew's birth.
She was nervous.

But it had nothing to do with Pete, she assured herself.
Because she wasn't interested in Pete...or any man. She
was nervous about her mother and Rafe. Especially because her mother was so excited. She didn't want her
mother to be disappointed.

"Kelly? May I come in?" her mother called.

"Of course, Mom." Kelly stood and headed for the
door as her mother entered. "Oh, you look so nice!"

"Thank you. I'm not too dressed up, am I?"

"No, that dress is perfect." The dress was a navy
print with small roses scattered around. The roses
matched the color in her mother's cheeks.

"You look beautiful, Kelly. Pete is going to be pleased." Mary beamed at her.

"Mom," Kelly said sharply. "You remember this date is just a pretense, don't you? I mean, you and Rafe aren't—but Pete and I don't—it's just a pretense, Mom."

She was afraid her mother would argue with her, but Mary only smiled and said, "But we can enjoy the movie. I haven't been to a film in ages."

Kelly smiled. "You can even enjoy the popcorn, Mom."

"I'd better get some money. I hadn't thought about popcorn. Mmm, I can smell it now."

"Mom, I think Pete can pay for your popcorn. After all, he owes us for helping him out."

Her mother seemed impressed with that idea, reminding Kelly that her mother had been on her own since she was sixteen. Kelly kissed her mother's cheek. "Just have fun, Mom."

"You should, too, honey. You don't ever get to have any fun."

The doorbell sounded at the outside stairs.

"That should be Lindsay. I'm glad she had the afternoon off since she's taking Drew home with her. He can be a handful."

"My grandbaby is perfect, and you know it," Mary scolded as she hurried to the door.

Lindsay followed Mary into the apartment. "Where's Drew?"

"Hello to you, too," Kelly said, grinning at her friend's enthusiasm for baby-sitting.

Lindsay blushed. "Sorry. But Gil and I are excited about Drew spending the night."

"Are you sure you want him to spend the night? He might wake you," Kelly warned.

"He'll be fine. Besides, you deserve to sleep in every once in a while. Since you're both dressed, do you mind if Gil and Rafe come up?"

"Of course not." Kelly said, noting her mother's panic. She crossed her fingers behind her back, hoping things worked out for her mother. Rafe was a nice man and her mother deserved some fun.

"Rafe's here?" Mary asked, her voice faint.

"Yes," Lindsay smiled as she answered. "He was too nervous to wait. Pete is going to meet all of you here so you can go in one car." She opened the front door and motioned down the stairs for the men to come up.

"I'll get Drew," Kelly said and slipped into her son's bedroom. She'd started him playing with his blocks, one of his favorite toys.

"Drew, Lindsay's here. Do you want to go play at Lindsay and Gil's?"

He stared at her, his blue eyes and brown hair just like her own. "Horsie!" he exclaimed. When they'd visited the ranch last Sunday, Gil had taken Drew to the barn to pat a horse.

"Very good, baby," Kelly exclaimed, proud of her child for making the connection. "Let's get your suitcase so you can visit the horsie again." She grabbed a small cloth bag she'd packed earlier and held out her hand to her son.

He stood and took her hand. "Horsie," he repeated.

She scooped him into her arms and hugged him close. "You're going to have a lot of fun, aren't you?" she teased with a laugh, hoping her child didn't notice the anxiety she was feeling about their separation.

"Of course he is," Gil said as he came into the room, obviously having overheard her.

She sent him a grateful smile, appreciating his encouragement.

"Hey, I thought he was a baby," another male voice exclaimed.

Kelly wheeled around to stare at Pete Crawford. She hadn't realized he'd arrived. "He is a baby!" she exclaimed, irritated by his remark.

"He's a growing boy," Mary said tactfully.

"Okay," Pete agreed, but his gaze was on Kelly. "Shall we go? The movie starts in fifteen minutes."

Kelly handed her son to Lindsay, then gave the suitcase to Gil. "If you change your mind about Drew spending the night, just call me. I don't mind coming to get him."

"We'll be fine," Lindsay assured her. She left the apartment, Gil following in her wake.

Kelly followed them so she could see Drew. When she turned to go back inside the apartment, she found the other three adults right behind her. "Oh! Are you ready to go? I have to get my purse."

"Here it is, dear," Mary said, holding out the black leather bag Kelly usually carried.

"But I need to—to put on lipstick," Kelly protested, hoping for a moment alone to collect herself.

"Put it on in the car," Pete said and grabbed her arm to pull her after him. "I don't want to miss the start of the show."

With Rafe and her mother waiting, too, Kelly didn't feel she had much choice. She accompanied her "date" down the stairs.

Pete drew a deep breath as Kelly slid into the front seat of his mother's sedan. He'd been afraid she'd insist on the back seat with her mother. Not that he'd mind. He didn't care where she rode, personally, but it wouldn't convince anyone they were interested in each other.

He got behind the wheel as first Mary, then Rafe, got in the back seat. "All set?" he asked cheerfully, hoping to make everything seem normal.

"Sure," Rafe returned.

In the rearview mirror, Pete saw Rafe help Mary with her seat belt. He checked to be sure Kelly had taken care of her own. The scent of her perfume drifted over to him. Her long dark hair seemed particularly enticing. When he'd seen her on Wednesday, it had been pulled back into a sedate braid.

"Uh, you're wearing your hair down," he muttered as he started the car.

She turned a startled gaze to him. "Does it matter?"

"No. It's—it's attractive." Dammit, he hadn't meant to say that.

"Compliments aren't necessary, Pete," she said in a low voice. "I agreed to do this. I keep my promises."

Her attitude irritated him. She needn't make it sound like an evening spent with him was torture. He glared at her.

"Anything wrong?" Rafe asked from the back seat.

"No," Pete assured him. "I hope we like the movie. It sounds okay."

Mary smiled. "It's been so long since I've been to a movie, I'm sure I will enjoy it." She smiled shyly at Rafe.

"I don't go often, either," Rafe assured her. "Mostly I like the popcorn."

Mary beamed at him. "Oh, me, too!"

Well, at least someone was going to have fun tonight, Pete thought to himself. He eyed his date out of the corner of his eye. She was sitting stiffly, eyes straight ahead. He figured he could pelt her with popcorn and she wouldn't notice.

There was a short line at the ticket box, and Pete figured standing in line would be a prime opportunity to make sure word got back to Sheila that he was "with" another woman.

"People are watching," he whispered to Kelly after they got in line. Then he casually draped his arm across Kelly's shoulders. She jerked away, then tried to relax. She even tried to smile. Pete hoped everyone else wouldn't notice her reluctance. Seeking a distraction, he stared at the advertisement for an upcoming movie. "Are you a Mel Gibson fan?" he asked, leaning closer to her.

"Um, he's okay," she replied, barely moving away.

"You're supposed to act like you like my company," he reminded her. "No one's going to believe that if you keep acting like I have the plague."

"I'm not acting like that!" she exclaimed even as she pulled back even more.

"Then why are you moving farther away?" he demanded.

"Because you're crowding me!" she snapped.

Exasperated, he said, "Did you think we could convince anyone by standing five feet apart? People who are attracted to each other touch!"

"But—" she began in protest. She stopped as a couple walked by, then stopped and came back.

"Pete!" the man exclaimed, sticking out his hand to shake. "I didn't see you for a minute. I thought you'd be with—"

The woman with him shoved her elbow into his ribs, stopping his words.

Pete knew his friend Mike was going to say Sheila. Her brassy blond hair drew the eye.

He nodded to the man's wife. "Hi, Marge. Do you know Kelly Hampton? Kelly, this is Mike and Marge Poston. They have a place south of ours."

"Oh, you're partners with Lindsay at Oklahoma Chic, aren't you? I've been hearing wonderful things about the store, even though I haven't been in yet."

Kelly thanked her for the compliment and started a conversation about fashion, leaving the men to talk alone.

"Sorry, Pete," Mike said. "I didn't mean to say the wrong thing. Have you and Sheila broken up? I heard you were pretty serious."

"You probably heard that from Sheila. I think she's ready to marry. That ticking-clock thing. But I'm a bachelor and I'm not wanting to change that fact."

The women had stopped talking and were looking at him.

Marge turned back to Kelly. "I hope you realize you're with a determined bachelor. I've overheard him say he never wanted kids, didn't I, Pete?"

Kelly gave a determined smile. "We're just seeing a movie tonight, not planning a lifetime."

An awkward silence fell. Finally the couple said goodbye and got in line behind several other couples.

Mary leaned forward. "You don't want any children?"

Pete hadn't realized Mary and Rafe had overheard their conversation. "Uh, Mary, I'm a bachelor."

"But—" Mary began.

"Mom, remember what we're doing," Kelly said softly. "We're pretending, remember?"

"I know, but it seems such a shame."

"Yeah," Rafe agreed.

Pete frowned at his friend. What was wrong with everyone? The whole point of the evening was to keep from falling into that trap.

"Sir, how many?"

He'd been slowly moving in the line, but he hadn't realized he'd reached the box office window. He turned around and asked for two tickets.

"What about Mom and Rafe?" Kelly asked.

"Rafe said he'd pay for him and Mary."

"But they're doing you a favor. You should—"

"Insult a man's pride?" he growled at her. Then he took the tickets he'd just bought and gently pushed her ahead of him into the theater.

"What do you mean?" she whispered.

"Rafe pays his own way, and Mary's, too, tonight. Popcorn?"

She studied him with those big blue eyes. "Can I pay for my own?"

He shook his head. "No. I have a little pride, too."

"Then no, thank you," she said and turned to see if Mary and Rafe were inside yet.

Pete stared at her in irritation. Rafe whispered to Mary as they came through the door. Mary moved to Kelly's side and Rafe headed for the refreshments counter. Pete followed him.

"I thought you'd be ahead of me," Rafe said.

"My *date* is being difficult."

"You two seemed a little cozy in line."

"I'm glad you thought so. I think we got the word out, anyway. Mike Poston's wife is friends with Sheila."

After Rafe got a bucket of popcorn and two drinks, Pete ordered the same and they returned to the women. Kelly took the drink he handed her with a brief thank-you, which was better than Pete had expected. Then she turned and followed Rafe and Mary into the darkened theater.

Once they were seated, the previews started. In the darkness, Pete put the popcorn between him and Kelly and leaned over to whisper, "I can't eat all this by myself."

Even in the darkness, he knew those big blue eyes were staring at him, but he kept his gaze on the screen. Without comment she took a few kernels of corn. As if he'd crossed a big bridge, he relaxed in his chair and slid his arm around the back of her chair.

"That's not necessary," she whispered, leaning toward him.

Her perfume filled his nostrils and he wanted to taste her. But he knew better than to get that carried away. However, he put his lips to her ear and whispered, "I'm not touching. It just looks that way."

She never looked at him, but she shifted slightly to create a little more distance between them. Stubborn woman, he thought.

When the feature film came on, he realized it was science fiction, not his favorite type of movie. With his eyes more adjusted to the dark, he checked out the people around them, recognizing several of Sheila's friends.

By the time the movie ended, he was much more interested in Kelly than the Hollywood beauty on the screen. She seemed plastic compared to Kelly's natural beauty. His arm had slipped gradually to rest on her shoulders. Once, she'd even cringed when the monsters seemed to jump off the screen toward them. He'd taken the opportunity to pull her close, her right breast pressing into his chest.

However, she recovered all too quickly.

When the lights came on, he leaned down and brushed her lips with his in a brief kiss, followed by whispering in her ear, "We're being watched."

She said nothing and Pete prayed no one managed to see the glare she sent him. He caught her hand in his. She tried to pull away, but she did resist discreetly. He held her fast.

Several more couples stopped and chatted on the way out, and Pete figured he was getting his money's worth. He decided it wouldn't hurt to lay it on thick.

"How about we stop at the ice-cream shop? Summer will be here before too long and I'm in the mood for a malt."

Mary smiled. "Oh, that would be—I mean, what do you think, Kelly?"

How could Kelly refuse another half hour, knowing Pete's suggestion had put the sparkle in her mother's eyes. But she wanted to. She felt he'd overstepped his bounds with that kiss. The one she liked too much. "A malt would be fun, if you have the time," she said, looking at Pete.

She knew why he'd suggested it. The front of the shop was all windows. Anyone arriving for the late show would see them. But the sooner Sheila knew about them, the less time she'd be involved in this charade.

Once seated with the promised malts in front of them, silence fell. Kelly tried to think of a subject that would engage both Rafe and Mary.

"Drew remembered seeing the horses when we visited last Sunday, Rafe."

"He sure liked them. Gil's real good with kids," Rafe responded.

"I think you'd be good with kids, too, Pete, if you'd try," Mary said, leaning forward.

"I doubt it," he said. Then he asked Rafe about his herd.

Before Rafe could answer, Mary tried again. "But children are so wonderful. Drew is an absolute delight."

"No, thanks," Pete replied, more bluntly this time.

"But you haven't—" Mary pushed.

Kelly tried to avert an ugly scene, but Pete was faster than she was.

"I already have a mother to nag on me about grandkids," he said fiercely. "I sure don't need another one."

Even Pete himself seemed appalled about his rudeness. Kelly supposed he'd opened his mouth to apologize, but she didn't wait to find out. She pulled her mother from her chair and walked out of the ice-cream parlor.

"I'm so sorry, Kelly," Mary apologized, tears in her eyes.

Kelly just kept walking. One of the few cabs in town was waiting at the movie theater, hoping to pick up a fare. Kelly opened the door and put her mother inside, following her as she gave the driver their address.

By the time the taxi started moving, Mary was sobbing. Kelly put her arms around her mother. "It's all right, Mom."

"But I've ruined everything!"

"Mom, there was nothing to ruin. It doesn't matter whether or not Pete likes children. It was all a pretense."

"But Lindsay said maybe you'd hit it off and—"

"I'm going to kill Lindsay," Kelly muttered. Her best friend had obviously convinced her mother this evening was a possible romantic moment for Kelly.

"No, I don't want to cause more problems!" Mary exclaimed.

Kelly sighed. "Don't worry, Mom. I didn't mean it. Everything's fine. But you have to promise you'll never try to persuade Pete he wants children ever again."

"I promise," Mary said, still weepy.

Pete was stunned by Kelly's reaction. He knew he hadn't been nice, but he'd been tense. And didn't the woman understand the whole purpose of the evening? It certainly wasn't to sell him on the idea of marrying and having a family.

He realized immediately he wasn't going to get any sympathy from Rafe, even before he spoke.

"What'd you go and do that for?" Rafe demanded. "I think Mary was crying. Come on, let's go after them."

Before Rafe could get to his feet, Pete stopped him. "It won't do any good, Rafe. I'm sorry I was rude, but

Kelly would hardly talk to me *before* I opened my mouth. Now she'll ignore me, or pull a gun on me.''

"I reckon you're right, but we should make sure they get home safely. They got in the taxi, and I've heard old Lenny takes a few nips of whiskey while he waits for a customer." He stood, waiting for Pete to join him.

Pete got up and followed Rafe out the door. "I'm sorry if I ruined your evening, Rafe. You and Mary seemed to be enjoying yourselves."

"You think she was having a good time?" Rafe asked anxiously, making Pete feel even worse.

"Yeah, I think so."

"She's a sweet little thing. Has the greatest laugh. And she even liked the movie."

"Yeah," Pete agreed and apologized again. "I'm afraid I got kind of tense and—well, I should've found a way to convince her I'm not father material."

"Why do you say that?" Rafe asked as he got into Pete's car.

"Don't you start on me, too. I'm trying to avoid marriage, not fall into the trap."

"Gil seems mighty happy."

"Good. I'm not Gil. I'll apologize to Mary, but I'm not going to take up fatherhood."

Pete set the car in motion. He could barely see the cab on the next block. He hoped Rafe had been wrong about what he'd heard. Pete would feel badly if there were an accident because of his rudeness.

The women were out of the cab and almost to the top

of the stairs when he stopped the car in front of their building.

"We'd better get up there to make our apologies before they go to sleep," Rafe urged.

"Maybe I should wait until tomorrow morning," Pete suggested as the women closed the door. "You know, I could bring flowers, do the apology right. That would be better, wouldn't it?"

Rafe stared at him. "You're stalling."

His succinct statement cut right through all Pete's words.

With a sigh, he said, "You're right. Okay, come on, let's go." He opened his door and got out of the car. He didn't want to face either Kelly or her mother again tonight, but he couldn't face his mother if he didn't. She'd be mortified if she heard of his behavior.

Rafe joined him as he stepped on the first stair up.

"I guess you won't ever forget this date, will you?" Rafe asked. "You ever been dumped before?"

"Not quite as efficiently. I don't think Kelly likes any man. Not just me. I wonder why?"

"You don't want to marry. I guess she has the same right," Rafe pointed out.

"Yeah, but I like women. I just don't want to marry one," Pete explained.

"You're spoiled," Rafe told him with a grin.

Suddenly the door to the apartment four steps up flew open, and both women poured out. Panic was written on their faces.

"What's wrong?" Rafe asked.

"Drew's in the emergency room!" Kelly practically screamed, trying to shove her way past Pete.

He grabbed her arm to keep her from falling. "Come on. I'll drive."

Chapter Three

Pete watched Kelly out of the corner of his eye as he sped toward the hospital. He decided he could've been a four-headed monster and she wouldn't have cared as long as he got her to her child.

Most of the young women he dated concentrated on either themselves or him. Kelly was only thinking of her child. She reminded him of his mother.

When he parked the car, she jumped out and was half-way to the emergency room before he could open his door. Mary hurried after her. Rafe waited for him to lock the door. Then the two of them followed the women.

"What do you think is wrong?" Rafe asked.

"Could be anything. Probably a broken bone. We had a lot of those while we were growing up," Pete muttered.

Inside, Kelly was talking to Lindsay and Gil, Mary

listening beside her. Then a nurse took Kelly away. Pete stared after her, feeling he should go with her, but he knew she wouldn't want him. He crossed to Lindsay's side. "What happened?"

"It's his appendix, Pete," a teary-eyed Lindsay said. "He was fussy, and I thought he missed Kelly. I tried to make him happy. Then he threw up! And—and he was running a fever. We called the doctor and he said bring him to the hospital!"

Gil put his arm around his wife. "It wasn't your fault, honey. We did everything we could."

Mary was fighting tears and Rafe had his arm around her, giving her strength.

Another nurse stepped forward. "Would you like to go up to the waiting room on the second floor? That's where the doctor will come after the surgery."

"Will Ms. Hampton go there?" Pete asked.

"Yes, sir, we'll send her there when she comes back."

Pete told the others to go upstairs and he'd wait here for Kelly. He didn't think she should come back by herself.

"Oh, thanks, Pete. That's a good idea," Lindsay said, patting him on the arm.

Pete leaned against the nurses' station counter, waiting for Kelly, wondering how dangerous the surgery was. He asked the nurses several questions. They said it was unusual for so young a child, but not too dangerous. He was feeling better about everything until he saw Kelly.

Silent tears streamed down her pale cheeks as she walked toward him.

She almost passed him, and he realized she wasn't seeing anything. He put an arm around her. "Kelly? Did you see Drew?"

Without answering, she turned and buried her face against his chest. He tightened his grip on her and buried his face in her hair. "Was he awake?"

She nodded, her sobs easing. "He was so frightened!"

"I know, honey. He's little, but he'll be okay."

He couldn't even understand the flood of protests she made, but he didn't need to. He remembered his mother when Mike, his youngest brother, had been in a car accident. He'd been pretty messed up. No one, not even his dad, had been able to comfort her until she saw Mike again and had the doctor tell her he would be all right.

"Come on upstairs. The others have gone to the waiting room where the doctor will come when it's over."

With his arm still around her, he moved them to the elevator.

She seemed surprised when they reached the waiting room and Lindsay and Mary ran forward to hear the latest about Drew. When she pulled away from Pete's warmth to hug them, he felt the loss. He wanted to protest and tell the other women that he could support Kelly better than them. He was stronger.

Eventually they sat down, and he took a chair nearby, with Rafe and Gil. There was little conversation. The men, all three of them, watched the women, ready at a minute's notice to do anything they could to help.

But there was nothing.

Finally Mary and Kelly got up. Mary explained they were going to walk the halls for a little while. Pete offered to accompany them and Kelly gave him a strange look, as if surprised he was there.

Mary shook her head, and Pete settled back in the uncomfortable chair.

Lindsay came back to Gil's side and he slid his arm around her. She put her head on his shoulder and closed her eyes. They made such a picture of oneness, Pete was surprised to feel envy. He'd seen it before with his parents. He'd even thought one day he might have that kind of relationship. But that was before he'd had experience with the opposite sex. An early engagement to a woman who was only interested in his money had filled him with cynicism.

As if to underline his decision about women, fun for a while but too difficult to understand, Lindsay suddenly raised her head and stared at her husband. Then she burst into tears and leaped from his side, running into the hallway.

"What happened?" Rafe asked.

"I don't know," Gil said, a stunned look on his face. "I just said I was glad it was Kelly's boy and not ours that was being operated on, and she went crazy."

"You don't care about Drew?" Pete demanded. Gil's words seemed harsh even to Pete, who claimed not to want any children.

"Of course I do. But if it was my baby, mine and

Lindsay's baby, I think I'd go crazy. That's all I meant.'' Gil stood. "I'd better go find her.''

Before he took two steps, Lindsay returned, Kelly and Mary with her.

"Honey, what upset you?" Gil demanded.

With a nudge from Kelly, Lindsay took a step toward him. "I—I thought you wanted a baby.''

Pete watched, wide-eyed, as Gil assured his wife. "Of course, I want a baby. I said that because it's hard when your own child—I mean, Kelly is suffering so much, I— why would you think I don't want a baby?''

"I wanted to baby-sit Drew tonight because—because I wanted to tell you—he's so sweet. I know you adore him and—I'm pregnant!''

Pete stared at his sister, then his friend. They were having a baby? He didn't know what to say.

Obviously Gil didn't, either. He stared at his wife as if he hadn't understood the words.

Rafe jumped up from his chair and hugged Lindsay, congratulating her.

His movement awoke Gil from his stupor. He hugged Lindsay tightly, whispering in her ear. Pete stood and added his congratulations.

"Are you sure?" Lindsay asked Gil. "When Pete was there the other day, you laughed and said—''

Gil and Pete hurriedly interrupted.

"I wasn't agreeing with Pete!'' Gil said in a rush.

"I didn't mean—I was just talking in general,'' Pete assured her.

Kelly stared at Pete, her gaze accusing him of some

heinous crime. "Really," he protested, "some women aren't—I mean, they don't—" He took another look at Kelly's stare and gave up defending himself.

Gil sat down and pulled Lindsay into his lap. They cuddled, whispering, and occasionally kissing, and the others sat in silence, trying to ignore them.

Finally Lindsay looked at her friend. "You were right, Kelly, he does want our baby!" She beamed at them all.

"Of course he does, Lindsay. Everyone knows he's crazy about you," Kelly assured her, smiling at both Lindsay and Gil.

Pete frowned. There was a bittersweet tone to her words and her expression that caused him to question her past. She had gotten married when she was pregnant, but Lindsay had assured the Crawfords that Kelly and her husband loved each other. Six months later, before she gave birth, he'd been killed in a rodeo accident.

Pete had assumed Kelly had refused to date anyone because she'd still been in mourning. Now he wondered.

"Uh, I imagine most men are excited about their first child," he said, watching Kelly closely.

After a hesitation, Kelly said, "Yes, of course."

She glanced down at her watch and looked back at the doorway, unconsciously reminding him of the ordeal she was going through. Yet she'd taken the time to help Lindsay.

It suddenly occurred to him that Lindsay's news would excite his mother. "Have you told Mom? She's going to be over the moon. You know how she wants a grandchild nearby." His brother Logan had one baby and another on the way but they were two or three hours away in Texas.

"Not yet. I had to tell Gil first," Lindsay protested.

"You've told him. Why don't you go call Mom and Dad," Pete suggested.

Lindsay and Gil jumped to their feet and hurried out of the waiting room after a quick word to Kelly.

Rafe suggested to Mary that they walk a little. He said his left leg went stiff if he didn't move around every once in a while. Mary leaped at the opportunity to nurse someone else, since she couldn't nurse her grandson.

Suddenly only Pete and Kelly remained in the waiting room.

He cleared his throat. "Thanks for helping Lindsay."

She was pacing the room, and she turned to stare at him. "I didn't do anything." She started walking again.

"Yes, you did. You calmed her down and got her to talk to Gil. I've never seen her that upset."

She paused again. "A woman is very upset during pregnancy. Her hormones are out of balance."

"Were you that way when you had Drew?"

Her eyes darkened, and she turned away, pacing again. He barely heard the "yes" she muttered.

"He's a cute baby."

She seemed surprised by his words, which made him feel defensive. He didn't hate children just because he didn't think he was cut out for fatherhood. He didn't think he had the patience a child needed.

"He's a little boy, almost two years old," she said.

Then she sank her teeth into her bottom lip and her eyes filled with tears. She quickly turned away.

Pete stood and put his arms around her. To his surprise she didn't protest. He figured tomorrow she'd slap him if he tried to hug her. But tonight, she'd hold on to any port in a storm.

"He's going to be fine, Kelly. Tomorrow, you'll be laughing about your fears."

She sniffed and muttered against his chest, "Maybe not tomorrow. It'll take longer than that."

"Yeah. How long will it take before you forgive me for what I said to your mother? I know I was rude and I apologize." He hadn't meant to bring up that subject, but he couldn't help himself.

To his surprise, even though she pulled away from his hold, she didn't seem angry. "I appreciate the apology, but Mom was at fault. Mom and Lindsay."

"What do you mean? Why would Lindsay—"

"Ms. Hampton?"

Both of them whirled around to stare at the doctor in surgical garb standing at the door.

"Yes! How is he? Is he all right? Is he awake? Can I see him?" Kelly asked.

Pete automatically put his arm around her shoulders in case she needed his support.

The doctor smiled. "He's fine, sort of awake, and yes, you can see him." When Kelly sprinted for the door, leaving Pete behind, the doctor took her arm and led her away.

That's when Pete noticed the doctor was a good-

looking man, and seemed to think Kelly needed him to
touch her. Pete knew the man wasn't touching her because of Drew. He was touching Kelly because like Pete,
he found her soft, charming, sexy—yet strong. The doctor wanted Kelly to lean on him.

Pete didn't agree.

Even though the doctor and the nurses assured Kelly
that Drew would sleep through the night, Kelly was determined to spend the night at the hospital. Her son had
awakened enough to recognize her, and she'd hugged
him and assured him his mama would be with him. She
was determined to keep her promise.

She returned to the waiting room and assured everyone that Drew was doing fine. Then she asked her
mother to bring her a change of clothes in the morning.

"You're staying the night?" Pete asked. "Is that necessary?"

"The nurses say it isn't, but I promised Drew I'd be
here when he woke up."

"But you'll be better in the morning if you get some
rest," he pointed out, logically, he thought. All three
women glared at him.

"What?" he asked.

"You just don't understand," Lindsay assured him.

"It makes sense," Gil said hesitantly, obviously worried about upsetting his wife again.

"When will he get to come home?" Mary asked, ignoring the men.

"The doctor said he might come home tomorrow, but

maybe they'll wait until Sunday. Oh! Lindsay, I won't be able to work tomorrow, our busiest day. Mom, can you help Lindsay? I'm sorry to ask but—"

"Of course I can," Mary said, straightening her shoulders.

"If it looks like we're going to be flooded, I'll get Mom to come in, too," Lindsay assured Kelly. "We'll be fine. You just take good care of Drew."

"Thanks," Kelly said, relief in her voice. Then she kissed her mother and turned toward the door.

"Kelly, I can stay if you need someone with you," Pete offered.

Everyone turned to stare at him and his face flushed.

Kelly was surprised by the warmth that filled her. She'd been alone since before her baby was born. And she knew Pete was trying to be nice, even if he didn't like children. So she appreciated his offer.

"Thank you, Pete, but I'll be fine."

She returned to her son's room and, after checking to see that he was sound asleep, she settled in the reclining chair and covered herself with the light blanket the nurse had left for her along with a pillow.

The nightmare was over. Her baby was safe again. She thought about Pete's words about recovering once she knew Drew was okay. She also thought about his broad chest and his gentle hold as he'd held her—and his offer to spend the night with her—and smiled. He was more of a comfort than she'd ever expected. She fell asleep at once.

* * *

Pete and Rafe dropped Mary off at the upstairs apartment. Rafe walked her to the door while Pete waited in the car. He'd been surprised at his reluctance to leave Kelly alone at the hospital. It didn't seem right. She appeared to be a strong woman. A dedicated mother. But she shouldn't have to bear the burden alone.

His mother was strong. But his father was always there for her. Gil would be by Lindsay's side all the way through the pregnancy. Kelly had been widowed when she was eight months pregnant. The more Pete thought about her alone, heavy with child, the more disturbed he became. And since then, she'd raised the child by herself. Only since she'd moved into the apartment over the store had she had her mother with her.

Had she loved her husband that much? Had she been devastated when he died? Tonight, for the first time, he questioned Kelly's reluctance to date. Two years was a long time to mourn so deeply.

Maybe he'd ask her, sometime, if—when he had a moment alone with her. Tomorrow, he'd go to the hospital to see the boy…and Kelly.

He rode out with his father and his brothers early the next morning on the Double C ranch. He mostly ignored the ribbing he'd taken about going out with Kelly. Finally he told them about Drew's operation. His father showed concern and immediately called his wife on his cell phone to tell her.

"She'd already talked to your sister. Lindsay asked her to come into the shop early today so Mary could go visit Kelly and Drew."

When his father got off the phone, Pete waited until his brothers moved away and said, "I'm going to take off in a couple of hours and go to the hospital."

His father's left eyebrow rose a little. "Going to take the little tyke some flowers?"

Pete hadn't thought about taking anything. "Uh, I might pick up a toy for him. I'll take Kelly some flowers."

His father looked amused.

"What?" Pete asked. It seemed he was asking that question a lot lately.

"You interested in Kelly?"

"No!" he exploded. Then he took a deep breath and said, "It just seems like the thing to do."

His father nodded and kneed his horse toward several cows standing under a tree. "It's getting hot already," he added, changing the subject.

Pete ignored that remark. "Dad, did Lindsay ever say anything about Kelly's husband?"

"She told us about the wedding...and the baby. We weren't invited because it was a hurry-up thing."

"You know anything about him?"

"He wasn't a star in the rodeo. As I heard it, he barely made a living. I hope he had insurance. Why all the questions? Does Kelly need help paying the bill at the hospital?"

"Damn! I never thought of that." Pete figured it was hard enough to have a child in pain without having to worry about how to pay for his care.

"We'll throw a fund-raiser to help her if you want. Your mother can organize something."

"I'll check with Lindsay," Pete assured his father. "I was asking because I assumed Kelly kept to herself because she loved her husband so much. Now I'm not so sure."

"I wouldn't know that, son. You'll have to ask Kelly. I know there was never any gossip or complaints about her behavior during her marriage or since."

"Was there about her husband?"

Caleb Crawford paused and stared at his son. "There was talk, but you'll have to ask Kelly if you want to know."

Then he turned his attention to the cows and Pete didn't ask any more questions. His father didn't repeat gossip when it was harmful to someone's reputation.

After a return to the house and a quick shower, Pete bought a toy airplane for Drew and a bunch of flowers in a vase for Kelly. He'd enjoyed shopping for the toy, but he'd been lost when it came to the flowers. The woman behind the counter at the hospital gift shop had suggested roses when she found out he was shopping for a woman.

He'd rejected the temptation. If everyone heard he was taking roses to Kelly, it would have helped his plan but it didn't seem honest. He wanted something to cheer her up, not make her mad.

It was enough that he was taking off work in the middle of the day to go see the two of them. Sheila worked at the hospital as a nurse. She'd hear fast enough about his visit.

He knocked on the partly closed door and waited.

"Come in," Kelly's smooth voice called.

He stepped into the room. "Good morning. How's Drew this morning?"

"Pete! I didn't expect—I mean, how nice of you to stop by. Drew's doing just fine, aren't you, sweetie?"

The little boy nodded, his eyes big, and Pete noticed how much they resembled Kelly's blue eyes. "I'm glad to hear it." He handed a gaily decorated gift bag to the little boy. "I brought you something to play with."

The little boy's eyes glistened with excitement, but he didn't move. Kelly reached for the bag. "That's very thoughtful of you, Pete. He doesn't move because it hurts. We've learned that lesson, finally." She smiled at him, and Pete basked in her welcome.

Drew put his hand in the bag when Kelly held it close to him and pulled out the airplane. "Airpane!" he exclaimed, leaving out the "l" in his pronunciation.

Kelly had him repeat the word correctly. Then she reminded him to thank Pete for his gift.

"You're welcome," Pete assured him. Then he held out the vase of flowers to Kelly. "I thought you might need some cheering up."

She blinked hastily and looked away as she took the vase. "Thank you," she added softly.

Was she crying? He hadn't done that much. "They're also to apologize for my behavior last night."

"Please, it wasn't—thank you," she said abruptly,

and turned her back to him to set the flowers on the bedside table. "Look, Drew, Pete brought pretty flowers. Aren't they nice?"

"Unbelievably nice," a female voice said.

Kelly and Pete both turned to find Sheila Hooten standing in the door, her hands on her hips.

Chapter Four

Kelly had been feeling warmer toward Pete. His kindness last night and today was appreciated. She didn't want any trouble with Sheila Hooten, but the woman did seem to appear frequently.

"Thank you for visiting us, Miss Hooten," she said, staring back at the woman.

"Oh, I'm not here for you, Ms. Hampton. I'm keeping track of what's mine." The hatred in the woman's voice was noticeable.

"What's yours?" Pete asked softly.

"You know you are, lover," Sheila replied, this time her voice as gooey as honey.

"No, I'm not, Sheila. I told you the first time we went out that I didn't want any kind of commitment," Pete said firmly.

"Well, I know, but I couldn't help falling in love with

you, Pete darling. Don't break my heart. I couldn't stand it." She came to his side and plastered herself against Pete.

He took her by the arms and moved her back several steps from his body. "Sheila, I'm not yours. I don't belong to anyone but my parents. Saying I am won't make that true."

"If you don't marry me, everyone will think you're a jerk. I told them all you asked me to marry you," she said calmly, triumph on her face.

"And I'm telling them differently. I'm interested in Kelly now, and a lot of people already know that. You're going to wind up looking crazy if you persist."

Kelly thought she could see smoke coming out of Sheila Hooten's ears as she suddenly glared at Pete. "Oh, yeah? Well, we'll see when I turn up pregnant." She spun around and marched to the door.

Pete stopped her. "Yeah, we will, because I won't marry you and I won't pay child support until I and the baby both take a paternity test."

She had halted to hear his response. Then she left the room.

"It looks like you waited too late for your plan," Kelly said softly, her gaze going to Drew's face to be sure the woman hadn't upset him.

"No, I didn't. I don't have unprotected sex. We were only together a couple of times and—"

"Condoms have been known to fail."

"Dammit, Kelly, she's not pregnant. Not with my baby!"

"Please mind your language around my son," she said, beginning to lose her sympathy for the man. He'd been kind last night and today, but that didn't stop him from being a jerk.

"I'm sure she just thought of that threat. But if she knows it won't force me to marry her, she won't get pregnant and try to blame me. We'll keep on with our masquerade until everyone believes I'm not interested in Sheila," he muttered, as if thinking out loud.

"I don't think that's a good idea."

"You mean you'd refuse?" he demanded, outrage in his voice. "You promised."

He had her there. She had promised to help him, for her mother's sake, but she hadn't known her child would be hospitalized. "I have to stay with Drew. Look what happened the one time I left him." Intellectually she knew Drew wouldn't get sick every time she left him with someone, but emotionally, she couldn't face doing so again anytime soon.

"He'll be well in a couple of days. It doesn't take long for kids to heal. I'll get Mom to volunteer to baby-sit. She's had a lot of experience with kids. Nothing can go wrong."

"I don't want to ask your mother to baby-sit. She's not family."

"She's my family. Lindsay isn't family, either, but it didn't bother you to ask her." His irritation seemed to be rising.

"Could we discuss this in a few days, after I have Drew home safe and sound?"

The door opened again. This time, the visitor was the doctor who had done the operation last night. Instead of being dressed in scrubs, he was wearing slacks and a sport shirt.

Pete glared at the man, which confused Kelly. What did Pete have against the man who had saved Drew's life? "Dr. Wilson, thank you so much for saving Drew." She left her son's side to shake the doctor's hand.

The doctor shrugged his shoulders and said, "It's my job, Kelly. How is he today?"

"A little sore, but doing well."

"If you don't mind, I'll look him over," the doctor replied, moving to the side of the bed.

"Of course not. Is it all right if I stay?"

"Of course."

She moved over by Pete while the man talked to Drew and gently examined him.

When he left Drew's bedside, he said, "He's doing well. Would you like to take him home this afternoon?"

"Oh, yes!" Kelly exclaimed, beaming at the doctor. "That would be wonderful."

"Okay, I'll write up his release papers. You'll need to keep him down for another couple of days, and bring him to see me in the office a week from today. Okay?"

"Yes, thank you, Doctor." She flew to the bed, telling her son the good news.

The doctor paused by Pete and stuck out his hand. "I don't believe we've met. I'm Dr. Patrick Wilson, new to Lawton."

"Pete Crawford." Pete wasn't anxious to get to know the handsome doctor. And he sure didn't want Kelly getting friendly with him. She needed another kind of man. An outdoor man. Someone like him, only not him.

"Are you the father?"

"No, just a friend." It would have been so easy to lie to the man, but he knew Kelly would straighten him out if he tried.

"I see. Glad to meet you."

His smile was pleasant, but he turned to watch Kelly with Drew, and Pete tensed again.

"I'll see you next week, Kelly...and Drew," he remembered to add just before he left the room.

"Seems like he's more interested in you than he is his patient," Pete said, trying to keep his voice cool.

"Don't be silly." With those words, she then ignored Pete. "Drew, Mommy is going to dress you now. But I'll be careful."

"I'll help," Pete announced. He'd never dressed a kid in his life, but he dressed himself on a regular basis. He figured it couldn't be too hard.

Kelly accepted his help gracefully, which surprised him. Her mother had brought a small set of warm-ups for Drew to wear. She let Pete hold the boy while she maneuvered the pants on over the diaper he was wearing.

"He still wears diapers?" Pete asked, surprised.

Kelly glared at him. "Drew was learning to be potty trained, but I figured it would be too hard for him right now. It hurts to walk, doesn't it, Drew? We'll worry about that next week."

She smiled at her little boy and Pete felt like a brute. He hadn't intended to hurt the little guy's feelings. He'd just been surprised.

After Drew was dressed, even his tennis shoes on his feet, Kelly said, "Play with your airplane while I call Grandma to come get us."

"Don't call her. I'll take you home," Pete said.

"I don't know how long you'd have to wait. I'd better call Mom."

"She's pretty busy at the store. When I went by, every parking space was full." He hadn't actually gone in the store, but he wasn't going to tell Kelly that.

"I'm sure Lindsay can spare her for a few minutes."

"Probably, but there's no need since I'm here. Besides, I thought pregnant women got tired in a hurry."

He watched her fight herself, the conflict visible in her features. But he figured he'd win. Kelly wasn't a selfish person.

Then she came up with another reason to turn down his offer. "But you don't have a car seat for Drew. It wouldn't be safe."

"Where is his car seat? I'll go get it."

"I don't know," she suddenly realized. "I gave it to Lindsay and Gil last night and—I guess they still have it."

He moved around her and picked up the phone. When Gil answered, he asked about the car seat.

"Yeah, we've still got it. Want me to drop it off today?" Gil asked.

"I'll come get it. Drew's going home today and

Kelly's worried about his safety." Now he had her. She'd have to go with him because he'd have the car seat.

"I'll bring it to the hospital at once," Gil promised. Before Pete could think of a reason to say no, he'd hung up the phone.

"The car seat will be here in a few minutes," he said to Kelly.

"Is Gil bringing it in?" she asked.

"Yeah."

"Well, I'm sure he'll be glad to drop me by the store. That way you won't have to wait."

"Dammit, I'm taking you home! Stop arguing with me."

"I believe I asked you to moderate your language around my child. And I don't think shouting at me is very nice."

"You're the one being unreasonable!" Pete returned, but as the door opened again, he realized he was definitely yelling.

Dr. Wilson looked at the two of them. "Is there a problem?"

"I'm just trying to take her home," Pete said stiffly, not looking at Kelly.

The doctor looked at Kelly. "Want me to call someone?"

Pete didn't know if he meant Security to have him thrown out of the hospital, or someone else to drive her home. And he wasn't sure what Kelly would say.

"No, I was being difficult, Doctor. Pete will take us home. Thanks again for letting us go today."

"Glad to do so. I'll see you next week."

As he left, a nurse came in, pushing a wheelchair. "Are we ready to go home, Drew?" she asked in a cheerful voice.

Kelly answered her question.

Pete stepped forward. "We don't need the wheelchair. I can carry him."

"Sorry, hospital policy." She pushed the chair up next to the bed. "Is he all ready?"

"Yes," Kelly agreed and reached for Drew.

Pete joined the crowd. "At least let me put him in the chair." He gently lifted the little boy and sat him down in the chair. He looked very small in the adult-size chair.

"Mama?" Drew said, his voice wobbly.

"I'm right here, baby," she hurriedly responded, kneeling down to talk to him. "You get to ride in this chair and I'll be right beside you. Then we'll ride in Mr. Crawford's truck and in no time we'll be home."

"You're taking them home?" the nurse asked Pete, surprise in her voice.

Pete knew Sheila had been busy spreading rumors around the hospital. In a firm voice, he said, "Yes, I am."

"Pete's a family friend," Kelly hastily added, making him angry again.

What was she doing? She was supposed to be pretending he was her boyfriend. He glared at her but it didn't seem to faze her.

"Pete, would you carry the suitcase while I hold Drew's hand?" she asked.

His answer was gruff, but he did as she requested.

"Grandma is going to be so glad to see you," Kelly chatted with her son as she accompanied his wheelchair out the door.

Pete followed after them.

When they got to the door of the hospital, he realized they had to wait for Gil's arrival before they could load Drew into his truck. Kelly had made it obvious she wouldn't go without the child seat.

He turned to the nurse to explain the situation when Gil called out to them. He was jogging across the parking lot carrying the seat.

"Thanks, Gil," he said, taking the seat from him. "I'll go put it in my truck and come pick you up," he added to Kelly.

"Hey, I could've—" Gil began.

"No! Just keep Kelly and Drew company until I get back." After all his struggle today, he wasn't going to let Gil take over now. Three minutes later, he pulled up in front of the hospital. He didn't see Kelly or Gil or the wheelchair. He left the engine running and got out, slamming the door behind him.

He charged into the hospital lobby and would have accosted one of the nurses behind the receiving desk, but Gil called his name before he could get out a question.

"Hey, pal, we went to get Drew a candy bar. You ready?"

Pete drew a deep breath. "Yeah. I was worried."

Gil grinned. "A hospital is a pretty safe place."

"Maybe," Pete said, staring at Kelly. He suspected she engineered the whole thing just to yank his chain.

When they loaded Drew in his seat, Gil told them he'd be following them to the store. He was worried about Lindsay being on her feet all day.

Kelly remained silent as they drove back to the apartment.

"Something worrying you?" Pete finally asked.

"I hadn't thought about the fact that Lindsay wouldn't be able to work as much. I'm not sure how we'll manage."

"Didn't you work when you were pregnant?"

"Yes, of course, but I didn't have a choice. I had to support myself."

"You were married, weren't you?" He frowned, the picture of Kelly pregnant with Drew, putting in long hours, bothered him.

"Yes. But Lindsay doesn't have to work long hours. Maybe we can hire a teenager to work the afternoons with me."

"Mama?"

"Yes, baby?" she answered in a distracted manner. It was clear she was still working out the logistics of the store.

"Airpane!"

Both Kelly and Pete paid attention. Pete was glad the little boy had liked his gift. She bent over and picked up the toy from the floorboard of the truck. "You'd better hold on to your toy or you'll lose it, Drew."

"I can buy him another." Pete thought he was reassuring the little boy. Doing something nice. Kelly turned to glare at him. What had he done now? he wondered.

"Why are you upset?" he asked.

"I don't want my son thinking he can be careless with his toy because someone will probably replace it. He needs to learn responsibility."

"He's only two, or almost, Kelly. I think you're being a little tough on him."

"Is that what your parents did for you? Replace anything you were careless with? Is that why you don't value important things?"

"What the hell are you talking about?" he demanded.

"Maybe that's why you don't value the love someone gives you. There'll be someone else along to love you."

"Don't you think you're getting carried away? We're talking about a toy airplane, not people," he exclaimed in exasperation.

Drew stared at both of them, worry in his gaze. "Airpane?" he asked, holding up the toy, as if to reassure his mother.

Kelly kissed him on the forehead. "Yes, sweetie, I know you have it. Good boy."

They'd reached the store and Pete saw a lady ready to back out of a front-door parking spot. He turned on his blinker and waited, ignoring Kelly as she ignored him.

After pulling in, he said, "I'll come around and get Drew."

"I can manage it," she murmured and reached for the door handle.

He reached out and caught her other arm. "No. I'll carry Drew upstairs. He's heavy and you don't want to have an accident. It would hurt him, as sore as he is." Ornery woman was driving him crazy. "Besides, I believe you've pointed out that I owe you."

"I didn't mean you had to take care of us."

"It's no big deal. Wait."

When he reached the other door, she had it open, but she'd remained seated with Drew in her lap.

He leaned in and scooped the little boy up, holding him against his chest. "Can you get down by yourself?" he asked Kelly. "It's a big step."

"Of course I can!" she assured him and slid down from the seat. Her skirt caught on the fabric of the seat and revealed her long legs, a view Pete couldn't help but appreciate.

Pete remembered to raise his gaze as she jerked down her skirt and she was glaring at him when he encountered her blue-eyed gaze.

"Sorry," he mumbled, not specifying whether he was apologizing for her difficulty getting out of his truck or for noticing her legs. It was the latter, of course, but he wasn't going to tell Kelly that. No way would he apologize for seeing those legs. He'd like to see Kelly in shorts...or nothing...visualizing his thoughts.

"Please move," Kelly said sharply. "I want to get Drew into bed."

Pete headed for the store. Kelly beat him there and held the door open.

The store was full of shoppers being tended by Lindsay, Mary and Carol Crawford. All three of them abandoned their customers to rush to Pete's side, greeting Drew.

Amid the questions, Kelly managed to tell Lindsay that Gil was on his way. Then she shoved Pete ahead of her to the stairs in the back.

Once they were upstairs in the apartment, she got Drew ready to take his nap. When he was tucked in, she turned to Pete. "Thanks for your help. I appreciate it."

"What are you going to do now?"

"I need to go downstairs and relieve Lindsay. Didn't you see how tired she looked?"

"But you haven't had it so easy the past two days. Why don't you take a rest first?" He knew last night and today had taken a lot out of Kelly.

"No. Lindsay is pregnant. She at least needs a break. I'd like to send her home, but I'm not sure I can do that. But she can come up here and rest." Without another word, she hurried down the back stairs. Pete followed her.

Downstairs, Gil was arguing with Lindsay, wanting her to go home. She was staunchly refusing, but now that Kelly had mentioned it, Pete could see Lindsay was pale.

Kelly stepped to her side. "Lindsay, why don't you

and Gil go upstairs? Gil can fix you a snack and you can put your feet up for a while. I'll feel better about leaving Drew alone if there's someone nearby.''

Pete knew Drew was sound asleep and Kelly had turned on the baby monitor but she was giving Lindsay a way to feel needed and yet still rest. Lindsay agreed at once, and knowing from past experience how stubborn his sister was, he was impressed with Kelly's success.

Pete knew his father would expect him to show up for the afternoon work, but he decided to stay at the shop. His mother showed him how to work the cash register, while she and Mary and Kelly handled sales. He even helped there, offering his opinion when the young women tried on dresses. They seemed to value his opinions over those of other females. He even advised one mother that the gown the girl wanted was too sexy for a young lady her age. The daughter was furious, but the mother was grateful.

Kelly stopped by his side after that transaction was completed. ''I hope you're being honest with these women.''

''Absolutely. That young lady had no business trotting around all exposed like that. That gown requires an older woman. It would look great on you,'' he added.

Her cheeks flamed and she stalked away. It was too tempting to believe his sweet words. She knew flattery didn't mean anything. But, oh, she wished it did.

Chapter Five

When Lindsay came downstairs a couple of hours later, she shooed her brother upstairs to keep Gil company. Her husband intended to stay until Lindsay could go home.

When Pete reached the apartment, Gil was sprawled on the sofa, watching a baseball game.

"Man," Pete said with a sigh, "selling clothes to fussy women is no easy task. I'd rather chase cows all day than stand around."

"I know. I'm thinking about forbidding Lindsay to work until after the baby comes."

Pete stared at his brother-in-law. "Let me know when you're going to make that mistake. I don't want to be in the vicinity."

Gil turned to look at Pete. "But I'm only trying to take care of her. That's my job."

"I may not understand women, but since Lindsay's come home, I've learned not to make choices for her. You'll regret it if you do that."

"You're wrong. She'll appreciate it," Gil insisted, but he was frowning.

Pete grinned. "Uh-uh. What are we going to do now? Just sit and wait?"

"I am. I don't know why you're waiting. This is where Kelly lives. She's already home."

Pete wasn't sure why he was staying, either. But he was reluctant to walk away. He searched for a reason to stay, one Kelly would believe—other than his need to be with her. Suddenly an idea struck him. "Hey, let's fix dinner for everyone!"

Gil stared at him as if he'd lost his mind. "Cook?"

"Not really, but we could bring food in. You know, get some barbecue, some potato salad, chips, a green salad. Then they can all sit down and eat. We'll call Rafe and Dad so when Mom and Lindsay get home, they won't feel they need to cook anything."

"Hey, that's a good idea. Do you think we can get it done in time?"

"Sure, if you'll go buy everything. I'll give you some money, but I need to stay here for Drew."

"Drew knows me. I wouldn't scare him," Gil protested.

"Okay, that would be better. 'Cause if anyone asks why I'm buying so much food, I can tell them I'm taking care of Drew and Kelly." Pete considered his plan to see if he'd left out anything.

Gil frowned. "Isn't that going to upset Kelly?"

"No, she promised to help me, but she doesn't want to go out yet until Drew's well. She'll like this alternative. Besides, she's exhausted."

Pete found a piece of paper and began making a list, including paper plates and cups so there wouldn't be any cleanup.

Gil insisted on giving him some money to pay half. Pete checked on Drew before he left, reminding Gil to keep an eye on the little boy and to call Rafe and his father.

It was almost six when he returned with everything they needed. He'd actually enjoyed himself, chatting with the grocery clerks and the owner of the barbecue restaurant. Each place he'd told them he was taking care of Kelly because of the rough time she'd had. He began to feel like a hero, as all the women told him he was.

His dad and Rafe were watching the end of the game with Gil. To his surprise, a drowsy Drew sat in Caleb's lap. But he looked up when Pete came in and held up his airplane. "Airpane!" he exclaimed.

"Right, buddy, airplane. Good boy! How are you feeling?" Instinctively he held out his arms and Drew reached for him. His father's face reflected his surprise.

"I didn't know you knew Drew that well. Just his mother," he said.

Pete ignored his surprise. "Yeah. I gave him an airplane."

Pete took him in his bedroom to change his diaper. He thought about his father's reaction. He supposed his friendliness was out of character for him, but Drew was Kelly's son. It felt right to take care of Drew. He came back in to direct the setting out of the food.

"Hey, Dad, you'd better go tell Mom to come up. She might head directly for the ranch wanting to get home and fix you dinner before she collapses."

"You could be right, son. By the way, this was a good idea, doing something nice for the ladies."

Pete grinned. Kelly was going to think he was wonderful. And that was a good thing.

After Caleb had gone downstairs, Rafe said, "I'm not complaining about getting to eat with Mary, either, Pete."

Pete knew that. Rafe seemed taken with Mary. With good reason. She seemed a very kind woman. Like her daughter.

The men arranged all the food on the kitchen counter, an impromptu buffet, and pulled up chairs for everyone. By then it was almost six-thirty. Pete stood back, ready to bask in Kelly's admiration.

Kelly was frowning when she came in the apartment. Drew's face lit up. "Mama!"

Pete was glad he'd picked up the little boy. It brought Kelly directly to his side.

"Hope you don't mind, Kelly, but we've taken care of dinner," he said, intent on making sure she noticed.

"What?" she asked, whirling around to stare at her kitchen.

"We knew you'd be tired. This way dinner is taken care of."

Kelly stared at all the people in her living room. Mary had just discovered Rafe and seemed pleased. Lindsay had come to sit by Gil and Pete's mother and father had been the last ones in. After a moment of silence, Kelly said, "Thank you for fixing dinner. That's very thoughtful."

But her voice wasn't overflowing with gratitude.

She clearly didn't see him as a hero.

He frowned, but what could he do? He urged her to fix a plate and sit down. He told her he'd feed Drew and snagged a chair next to her. Then he asked how business had been the past couple of hours.

Lindsay enthusiastically answered that question. It had been wonderful. They had overflowed and had made a lot of money. "I think we may need to expand."

His father and Gil warned against sudden expansion, but Pete said nothing.

Neither did Kelly.

Drew ate his dinner well. Pete knew Kelly was watching him to be sure he didn't harm her son, but eating was something Pete was an expert about. When Drew finished, looking sleepy again, Pete picked him up and left the room.

Kelly immediately followed. "What are you doing?"

Pete thought of several responses. She was so suspicious, not trusting him to do anything right. But he simply said, "I'm giving him a bath and dressing him for bed. He's already sleepy."

"I'll do it. Go finish your meal."

"I did. Go put your feet up. You look tired."

"Gee, thanks. That makes me feel better."

"Dammit, Kelly, I'm trying to help and you act like I'm planning a sneak attack!"

"I told you to quit saying that in front of my son!"

He took off Drew's wet diaper and headed for the bathroom. Drew didn't protest. He liked baths, Pete discovered when he splashed him and giggled.

"You don't know anything about bathing him!" Kelly warned.

"Baby, water, soap. What's to know?"

"Nothing, but—be careful around the staples they put in," she finally said.

Pete, however, had made it a fast bath and scooped Drew up, wrapping him in a towel. "Come on, cowboy, time for your pj's."

"Don't call him that!" Kelly insisted.

Pete turned to stare at her, reviewing what he'd said. "Do you mean cowboy? Don't call him cowboy?"

"Yes! Yes, that's what I mean. He's not a cowboy. He's not going to be a cowboy. Ever!"

He'd been wondering why Kelly seemed to dislike him so much. He'd never done anything to Kelly. He was trying to be nice and she kept complaining. "Is that why you don't like me? Because I'm a cowboy? Are you a snob?"

"No! I don't— My husband was a cowboy." She stopped and turned to leave the room.

"Aren't you going to tell your kid good-night?"

That question stopped her. She came back to the bed

to help finish putting Drew into his pj's. "Good night, sweetie. I'm glad you're home tonight."

Drew had managed to grab his airplane from the bed where he'd left it before they went to the bathroom. "Airpane!"

"Yes, you have your airplane. Good boy. Maybe one day you'll fly an airplane. Do you want to be a pilot?"

Drew snuggled down with his airplane, a smile on his face, probably not clear about what his mother said.

Pete, however, had a lot of questions.

"What did your husband do to you?"

Kelly kissed her son good-night and headed for the door, ignoring Pete's question.

"Kelly, I want to know."

She stopped when he reached out to catch her arm. But she wasn't interested in talking. "Number one, I'm too tired tonight to talk to anyone. It was kind of you to arrange a meal, but I need to go to bed, now. Number two, my marriage is my business and not yours. I may be pretending to be your love interest for the moment, but we're just pretending. You don't have the right to ask me questions!" Then she pulled free and went to join the others.

Pete followed, drawing the door softly closed after noting Drew's instant surrender to sleep. He couldn't argue with her rationale, but he wanted to. He might not be in love with Kelly—she irritated him too much—but he respected her. She was a good friend to his sister. She sacrificed her own exhaustion for Lindsay. She would do anything for her son. She maintained her independence instead of leaning on a man.

And he wanted to know why she hated cowboys.

Another look at her pale face and he began packing the leftover food into the refrigerator and throwing out the used plates and cups. Mary helped him but there wasn't much to do. Then he urged his parents out the door and nodded to Gil for his family to follow.

Outside, he turned back to look at Kelly standing in the doorway. He wanted to tell her he intended to ask his questions again when she wasn't so tired, but he didn't. He figured she knew him that well. He'd be back.

Kelly didn't leave the apartment until early Monday morning. Rafe asked Mary to go to Sunday dinner with him. She offered to stay home with Kelly and Drew, but Kelly encouraged her to go with Rafe. Kelly and her son spent a lazy day resting. Except during Drew's nap when Kelly vacuumed the store. She didn't want Lindsay vacuuming anymore.

Kelly felt refreshed when she rose on Monday morning. After an early breakfast with Drew and Mary, she headed to the grocery store. She wanted to be back by nine, when Lindsay was coming in. They needed to discuss how much Lindsay would work. And decide if they needed to hire a teenager to help.

"I could go to the grocery store for you," Mary offered.

"That's okay, Mom. Actually it feels good to return to my routine after the past few days. If Lindsay gets back before I do, fix her something to drink so she won't start work.''

"Will do. I'm so excited about her baby. Rafe is, too.''

"Really? That's good. By the way, you didn't say much about your date yesterday.'' Kelly had asked her when she got home, but Mary hadn't wanted to talk.

Though her cheeks turned rosy, Mary shrugged her shoulders. "Oh, we just ate and talked. Nothing exciting.''

"Okay,'' Kelly said, letting the conversation die. She wasn't going to force her mother to talk. She grabbed her handbag and headed for the grocery store.

When she went to check out, after piling her cart high, she discovered that her shopping wasn't routine.

"Kelly! You need this much food after everything that Pete bought for you Saturday?'' the checker, a friend from high school, asked.

Kelly stared at her. "How did you—I mean, there were a lot of us to eat that food. There's not much left now.'' She wanted to protest, but she figured the less she protested, the sooner it would fade from memory.

"Well, don't worry. I'm sure he'll buy you some more. After all, the Crawfords got a lot of money.''

That made Kelly mad. She'd worked hard to support herself and her son, to be independent. "I don't need anyone to buy me food, Betty Sue. I'm doing just fine on my own.''

"I heard your store is really doing good. Must be nice to be your own boss.''

Kelly only said, "Yes," not mentioning the long hours and barely scraping by until Lindsay became her partner.

"You're as lucky with men as you are with your business, too. After all, you married James Hampton. He may not've been rich, though I heard he did pretty well on the rodeo circuit, but he was a handsome thing. And now you've stolen Pete right from under Sheila's nose. He's handsome *and* loaded."

Kelly knew she was reaching her limit. One more comment like that and she'd explode. She went to the end of the counter and began putting the groceries in plastic bags.

"Sorry we don't have anyone to help you with that. They're all in school."

"That's all right. Do the high schoolers you hire work out all right? We may hire some part-time help."

"Really? I know several girls who'd love to work there. They figure they can spend all their salary at the shop."

"I like the sound of that," Kelly said cheerfully, relieved that the conversation wasn't about her or Pete anymore. "Anyone who might be interested can—"

"Well, lookee here. I guess you don't need any help after all," Betty Sue said, beaming over Kelly's shoulder.

She whirled around to find Pete walking in the automatic doors, smiling at her.

"You come to carry Kelly's groceries, Pete?" Betty Sue called.

"Sure," Pete agreed. "That's why I'm here."

"You're spending more time these days chasing after Kelly then you are them cows," the checker said. "Your pa is gonna have a fit."

Kelly hadn't said a word since Pete came in. Now she sped up her sacking, keeping her head down. She saw Pete's hands pull an empty buggy over and start putting her plastic sacks of groceries in it, but she still kept quiet.

Betty Sue didn't seem to notice. "I tell you, Pete. I'm glad you dumped Sheila Hooten and took up with Kelly. That Sheila's no good. Kelly, here, is as good as gold."

While she talked, Betty Sue had finished ringing up the groceries. Kelly pulled out her checkbook to pay as quickly as possible.

"Here. Let me get that," Pete suggested, his deep voice a sexy rumble.

Kelly was sure many women would consider it attractive, but it grated on her nerves. "No! I'll pay for the food." This time she looked at him, hoping her gaze conveyed her anger.

It must have, because he took a step backward and apologized.

She handed the check to Betty Sue. As she did so, Pete put the last of the groceries into the basket and turned it to the door.

"See you, Betty Sue," he called out and pushed it toward the door, not waiting for Kelly.

"You'd better hurry and catch that man," Betty Sue whispered. "He's a jewel."

Kelly gave a brief nod and hurried after Pete. She didn't know if Betty Sue was telling her to catch up with Pete this morning, or catch him in marriage. Either way, she wasn't interested!

"Why aren't you at work?" she demanded as Pete reached her old station wagon.

He ignored her question. "You gonna open the back so I can unload the groceries?"

She considered telling him no, but that would be silly. Opening the back, she stood there in silence watching him easily unload the groceries. She even sighed as she thought about carrying the groceries up the flight of stairs at home. But she knew Mary would come help her. They would manage.

As soon as the bags were loaded, she gave him a brisk thank-you and got in the station wagon. He didn't complain about her lack of friendliness, which made her feel guilty. But she'd had about all of Pete Crawford she could handle this morning.

She realized she wasn't finished with him when she discovered him following her in his big pickup. Was he going to carry the groceries up the stairs? She wouldn't complain. It would be in private, so everyone wouldn't be congratulating her because she had her claws into a hunk. A rich hunk.

He got out of the truck, and came to the back of the station wagon. "Do I dare offer to carry the groceries up the stairs, or are you going to snap at me?"

"It's not necessary," she replied stiffly. She knew he was referring to her bad manners at the grocery store.

He grinned and reached inside for a few of the bags. "Why don't you go on up and unlock the door? I'll take care of these."

She didn't argue with him, but she collected three of the plastic bags before she climbed the stairs. Mary opened the door before she got up there.

"How nice of Pete to help you!" she exclaimed with a smile.

"Did you tell him where I was?"

"Yes. He said he needed to talk to you." Mary took the bags from Kelly and carried them to the kitchen cabinets.

With a sigh, Kelly headed back down the stairs, turning sideways as Pete went past her, loaded with groceries. She gathered three more bags and turned, only to run into Pete's body. He'd made an extra fast trip.

He took the three bags from her and then added the last two. "Go on up. I've got these."

A car drove by and the driver leaned out the window to wave and call hello to them.

Pete waved back. Kelly nodded, but she wasn't enthusiastic. The driver was one of the worst gossips in town. In no time, it would be all over that Pete took off work to help Kelly do her grocery shopping.

There wasn't anything to be done about it, however. She turned and started up the stairs again, Pete on her heels.

"How's Drew this morning?"

"He's doing much better," she said. It had been a

relief when Drew woke up this morning, cheerful and hungry.

"Good. Does he still have his airplane?"

"Yes, thank you. It was generous of you to buy him a toy."

"Hey, I wasn't asking so you'd praise me, Kelly. I was afraid he'd lost it."

"He hasn't lost it." What else could she say? He said he didn't want to be praised. She was happy to accommodate him.

Mary was putting the groceries away already, while Drew sat on the couch and watched *Sesame Street*. Much to Kelly's relief, Pete joined Drew on the sofa and left the putting away of groceries to her and her mother.

Just as they finished, Lindsay knocked on the inside door that led to the store.

"Morning," she greeted them as she came in. Then she noticed her brother on the sofa. "Pete? What are you doing here?"

"One of the tractors broke down and I came in to town to get a new part. It won't be ready until two o'clock. I thought I'd check on Drew until then."

"Is he doing better?" Lindsay asked, moving to the sofa.

"Yes, much," Kelly answered. Thanks to Lindsay, she now knew why Pete was here. And learned that she had five more hours before he'd be leaving, too.

But she'd be busy in the store. He wouldn't bother her.

"Good. Uh, we need to talk this morning," Lindsay said, sounding worried.

"Yes, I thought we should. I was discussing hiring a teenager with Betty Sue this morning. She said she knew several who would love to work here and would spend all their wages in the store."

"You're not going to work anymore?" Pete asked, surprise on his face.

Lindsay's jaw squared. "Yes, I am," she said firmly. "But maybe not as many hours. I want to talk to Kelly about it, though, not you!"

Pete held up a hand. "*I'm* not trying to interfere. It was Gil who said—uh, I mean, he was concerned."

Lindsay gave her brother a hard stare and turned toward the door. "Maybe we'd better talk downstairs, Kelly."

Kelly looked at Pete. "Pete, it would be better if you left. Lindsay and I need to sit here and have a cup of tea, so she won't get tired."

"How about we talk first, then I'll leave."

"We who?" Kelly demanded.

"You and me. Maybe Mary can go down and help Lindsay until you get downstairs."

"I won't have you organizing my work schedule. The shop is none of your business!" Kelly returned.

Lindsay, however, said, "I think that will work. I'll be ready for a break by then and Mary will have everything set up. She can run the store for half an hour while we talk. But you've only got half an hour, Pete."

Before Kelly could protest, both Lindsay and Mary started down the stairs, pulling the door closed behind them.

Chapter Six

"I don't understand what we have to talk about," Kelly said sharply. She raised her chin, as if preparing for the worst, and took a step back.

Pete figured she was lying, but he'd play along.

"You don't?"

"I know I wasn't very…friendly at the grocery store, but I've worked hard to be independent. It angered me that you thought you should pay for my groceries. And that Betty Sue expected it, too. Especially after Saturday."

"What do you mean, especially after Saturday? I thought you'd be pleased that you didn't have to cook." He'd wondered about her reaction. He'd decided it was because he was a cowboy and she hated cowboys. Now she was giving him another reason.

She nibbled on her full bottom lip and Pete's gaze

zeroed in on that action. The woman never tried to tempt him or act sexy on purpose. He guessed she was a natural, because he sure wanted to sample those lips, to feel her soft, naked flesh against his. To hold her as he did in the hospital.

"It was a thoughtful gesture, but…but it was an expensive one, and I don't like to feel like I owe someone."

Since most of the women he dated wanted him to pay for everything and more, if they could convince him to buy them expensive presents, he studied Kelly. "You don't?"

"No. I take care of me and my family."

"So do I." After she turned and stared at him, he added, "and whatever woman I'm with."

"Well, you're not 'with' me. We're pretending, remember?"

"I remember, but I don't want to telegraph that to everyone in Lawton. I'm too well-known. If I don't buy you things, people won't believe our pretense."

She slumped into a chair and covered her face. When she took her hands down, she said, "I think we should give up this pretense. Sheila didn't sound like she was going to give up. Maybe you should just find some woman you can marry and be done with it!"

"Okay." He was irritated when she cheered up. He knew what else he had to say wasn't going to make her happy. "Ready to go get the license?"

When his words finally hit home, she leaped to her feet, her hands on her hips. "Not me, you idiot!"

He sat down, as if his knees gave way. "Well, I do believe my sister was right."

Still agitated, Kelly demanded, "About what?"

"You really *don't* want to marry. Just like me."

"More than you," she snapped. "I've already tried it before, remember?"

Now they were getting to the real topic he'd wanted to discuss. "Oh, yeah. The cowboy."

"Cowboy!" Drew exclaimed, peeking over the top of the couch.

Pete had forgotten the little tyke was in the room with them. He grinned at the little boy. "Yeah, cowboy. He rides horses," he added.

"Horsie!" Drew said, his grin widening.

"No!" Kelly protested. Then her voice softened. "Baby, do you want some milk and cookies?"

"I do, too," Pete said, trying to look needy. He saw the frustration on her face, but he still wanted some answers.

She glared at him, but he stood to help Drew to the table. Finally she got out the milk and poured two glasses, a tippy cup for Drew and a large glass for Pete. Then she put two saucers on the table. She added three cookies to each saucer.

"Thanks, Kelly. These look great."

She didn't even acknowledge his good manners.

"Are we through?" she demanded.

No, he wasn't through, but he decided he wasn't going to get any answers out of Kelly. Maybe he should go an indirect route. He knew Lindsay would have some answers. And she may have shared them with Gil. His friend wouldn't think anything about passing them on.

"We need to plan our next outing."

"I can't go until Drew's well," she hurriedly assured him.

"He looks well to me." He studied the little boy who grinned at him, cookie crumbs on his face, his saucer empty. "His appetite is sure good."

"Yes, but—I can't leave him with someone until after his checkup. If the doctor says he's okay, then we'll decide something."

"What time's your appointment on Thursday?" he asked, remembering the doctor's orders.

"Ten o'clock."

"Okay, I'll wait till then if you'll let me go to the doctor's office with you."

"No! That will make it look like we're—"

"A couple?" He waited silently. When she said nothing, he reminded, "You promised."

She lowered her head. "I know. Okay, but nothing until Thursday."

Nothing planned. But he might visit the patient, say, Tuesday evening. That wouldn't be planned. And it would keep their togetherness on everyone's mind.

"I've got to get downstairs. If you need somewhere to wait until your tractor piece is ready, you can stay here. But I have to work."

"I appreciate that, but I've got a couple of errands to run. Thanks for the offer, though. That's right neighborly of you."

She stood there staring at him, blinking her eyes, and Pete wondered if she was flirting with him. Until he saw the sheen of moisture in her eyes. She was upset?

"What's wrong?" he asked, taking a step toward her.

"I—I was rude this morning and you're being very nice about everything."

"Aw, shucks, that's the way cowboys are, honey," he said, grinning. Then he leaned closer and brushed her lips with his. Before she could protest, he leaned over and kissed Drew's cheek, cookie crumbs and all, and strode out the door.

Kelly remained standing there, staring at the door, trying to clear her head. It wasn't that he hadn't kissed her before. He had. But they'd all been performances. But this morning, they were all alone. The only one to impress was Drew. And still he'd kissed her. A sweet, gentle kiss. One that made her want more. She was discovering a big difference between Pete and her so-called husband.

Pete had forgiven her rudeness this morning and told her it was what cowboys did. Obviously he didn't know many cowboys. Which was a ridiculous thought. Before he'd left for the rodeo, James had gotten irritated with her and slapped her hard. That was the morning he'd left. She'd known then that she couldn't stay with him. But she let things drift since he was gone.

And he called himself a cowboy.

She cleaned Drew's face and hands and scooped him up. "Let's go down and see Grandma and Lindsay, okay?'' She needed to counteract Pete's testosterone with some feminine company.

Lindsay was just opening the front door for a customer waiting on the sidewalk. It was a couple of minutes early, but that was okay. Since there was only one customer, Lindsay turned her over to Mary and met Kelly at the bottom of the stairs.

''I think it's safe for us to go up,'' Lindsay said.

''Okay. Mom will give us a call if it gets crowded.''

Back upstairs, Kelly put Drew on a play mat in his room, leaving the door open, and set out his blocks. Then she rejoined Lindsay at the kitchen table.

''Mmm, cookies,'' she murmured, looking at the one left on Pete's plate.

''Here, I'll get you some and a glass of milk.''

''Aren't you going to have some?''

Kelly decided she deserved a reward after her trying visit with Pete. ''Yes, I am,'' she said firmly, ''but I'll have Diet Coke with mine so I don't feel so guilty.''

''Good thinking,'' Lindsay agreed with a laugh. ''I miss caffeine, but I want to do what's good for the baby.''

After Kelly sat down, Lindsay said, ''Gil read me the riot act last night, saying I needed to stop working until after the baby's born.''

''Of course, I can—''

''No! You don't understand. Gil was way out of line.''

''But, Lindsay, he's only trying to protect you.''

''Yeah, he used that line, too. But he needs to trust

me. I'm not a simpleton. If I get tired, I'll rest. I can go
upstairs and lie down and get Mary to come down, so I
don't think we need any extra help.''

"I know Mom would be glad to help you out like
that. And she'd like to make a little more money. But
I've been thinking about hiring a teenager. We are getting some younger clientele, but I think hiring a couple
of teenagers to work a few hours each week would be
great advertising.''

"You think so?''

"I do. And I'm mad I didn't think of it before. Teenagers don't read the newspapers. They're going to learn
about our store from their peers. And we are making
good money now, aren't we? We don't have to have one
of us on the floor all the time. Especially with me right
upstairs, close at hand if there's a problem.''

"That's true,'' Lindsay said slowly. "I think you may
be right. And when I deliver, if we have trained help I
wouldn't feel so guilty about taking time off.''

"Exactly!'' Kelly exclaimed, smiling.

"Now why didn't Gil explain everything this way.
Then we could've avoided a massive argument.''

"Because he's a man,'' Kelly said simply.

Both women laughed. Then Lindsay said, "Did your
discussion with Pete go any better? What did he want?''

Kelly realized she wasn't sure. "He was cooperative.
He wanted to schedule our next outing, but I asked him
to wait until after the doctor clears Drew.''

Lindsay raised her eyebrows in surprise. "Well, good
for him.''

"Kelly, come down," Mary said calmly over the intercom.

Kelly pushed the button. "On my way." Then she turned to Lindsay. "Why don't you take a fifteen-minute rest on the sofa while Drew is playing so nicely. Then you can come down and work until noon when I think you should go home."

"But I will have hardly worked at all. I can stay until two. That will be better."

"We'll see," Kelly said and hurried down the stairs.

Gil and Rafe were in the Mother barn, what they called the barn that had the mares near their time, when Pete arrived at Lindsay's home. Rafe stepped out when he heard a vehicle.

"Hi, Pete. We're in here."

Pete entered the barn at a leisurely stroll. He knew if he was going to get information out of Gil, he'd have to make him think it didn't matter. "Hey. How's it going?"

To his surprise, Gil looked outraged. "What are you doing here? If you're here to say I told you so, just go on home."

"Now, boy," Rafe said softly, obviously trying to soothe Gil.

Pete didn't need any enlightenment. "Well, no, that's not why I'm here. I didn't know about your argument until this morning, and I figured you got beat up enough by my dear little sister."

"I was just trying to take care of her!" Gil protested.

It was a struggle for Pete to stop from saying "I told you so," but he kept quiet.

After his outburst, Gil stood there, hands on his hips, his head hanging low. Finally he looked at Pete. "Thanks for not saying it."

Pete nodded. "Your heart was in the right place."

"She got so upset she yelled at me!" Gil added, amazement in his voice. "I've never seen her like that."

"We tried to tell you before you insisted on marrying her," Pete said with a grin. "But you were determined."

"But what I don't understand is why?"

"She wants to make her own choices," Pete said, pointing out what he'd said on Saturday.

"I don't think either one of you get it," Rafe said, leaning on his pitchfork. He'd been cleaning out stables.

"What don't we get?" Gil asked, irritated. "You said you didn't understand women. How would you know the answer?"

"Because I know how I'd feel."

"How's that? You're not a woman." Pete tipped his Stetson back, waiting to hear Rafe's words of wisdom.

"*I'd* think you didn't trust my judgment. Even worse, I'd feel you think I'd be selfish enough to do something to hurt the baby."

Gil stared at his best friend, alarm on his face. "Of course I wouldn't think that of Lindsay. And I trust her!"

"How would she know that?" Rafe asked.

"She should know he's only trying to protect her," Pete insisted, but he was thinking about Kelly's protests about his offering to buy her groceries. Did she think his offer meant he didn't think she could pay for them? Did she see that as an insult?

"So, even though you don't understand her, she should automatically understand you?" This time Rafe was grinning at Gil.

"Damn! I've been blaming her for everything," Gil muttered. "I thought I was in the right completely. Now I realize I've been a jerk. Is she going to forgive me?" he asked Rafe.

"I guess she will, 'specially if you get down on your knees, apologize and explain why you said those things. And maybe cook dinner tonight."

As if in a daze, Gil wandered out of the barn without even saying goodbye to Pete.

"Man, he's got it bad," Pete said, thinking he'd lost his opportunity to get any information. Then he looked at Rafe speculatively.

"Yeah, and someday it will happen to you," Rafe said with a grin.

"Has it happened to you?" Pete asked, watching the man.

His cheeks turned red. "A couple of times."

"Why haven't you married, then?"

"The first time, she loved someone else." Rafe stopped there and dug into a bale of hay with his pitch-fork.

But Pete wasn't letting him stop there. "And?"

Rafe tossed part of the hay into an empty stall. Then

he looked at Pete. "And the second time...I'm working on it."

"You mean Mary?"

"Yeah."

Pete watched Rafe work for a minute. Then he said, "If she's as hardheaded as her daughter, I'd say you've got a difficult time ahead of you."

Rafe rested on the pitchfork and looked at Pete. "Mary's not as...as angry as Kelly. She's mellowed over the years, though neither of them picked winners. Or was picked by. Mary says she got lucky because the bastard that got her pregnant didn't hang around."

"Has she talked about Kelly's husband?"

"Yeah." Rafe started working again.

"Rafe, Kelly says she hates cowboys. Doesn't want Drew to grow up to be a cowboy. I just want to know why."

"Can't you figure it out, boy? Her husband, and I use that word loosely, called himself a cowboy."

"But what did he do?"

"You name it, he did it. He got her pregnant, married her and then hightailed it to the rodeo, leaving her to face everything alone. If that wasn't enough, he hit her before he left town. Then he spent every penny he earned on women and drink and asked for her hard-earned money to pay his fees."

Pete felt sick to his stomach. Kelly was the most generous woman he knew. And the hardest working. No woman deserved that kind of treatment, but least of all Kelly. "I see," he said grimly.

"Yeah, I thought you would."

"But she stayed married to him?"

"She was going to divorce him as soon as Drew came. Until then, her lawyer advised her to wait."

"I hope he had a big insurance policy," Pete muttered.

"Nope. He hadn't paid the premiums, though he'd promised. There was a small policy the rodeo required, but it wasn't much. And he left debts."

"Damn!" Pete said under his breath.

"I told you all that because if she's hurt again, Mary's gonna be upset. And so will I." There was a threatening tone in Rafe's last words.

"So that will make three of us," Pete said clearly. "But that doesn't mean I'm going to let her paint all cowboys with that jerk's stripe."

"I can understand that. Just don't lead her on. We both know you aren't interested in anything permanent. Make sure she keeps that idea in her head."

Pete nodded. Of course he wouldn't lead her on. He'd never—he remembered the kiss. It had been a little one. It wouldn't count for anything. Kelly wouldn't think anything about it.

You did, a little voice reminded. He'd thought about it all the way to Gil's. He suddenly promised himself he wouldn't do that again. He wouldn't touch her unless he had to to carry on the pretense. After all, he was a true cowboy, honest, trustworthy, kind and protective of what was his.

And Kelly wasn't his.

Rafe seemed satisfied. "Good. Let's go make some sandwiches. I'm ready for lunch."

"Hey, I didn't mean to invite myself for a meal," Pete protested, embarrassed.

"Don't be silly, boy. I owe you for Saturday night. I took Mary to lunch yesterday. It was easy to ask her Saturday night, but I would've been in trouble if I'd had to get up my nerve to call her." He nudged Pete toward the barn door with a grin.

"Okay," Pete agreed, smiling back.

When they got to the house, Gil was hanging up the phone receiver, a silly grin on his face. "She's not mad," he announced, as if he'd made an incredible discovery.

"She wasn't?" Pete asked, surprised. "Are you sure? 'Cause Lindsay can fight dirty."

Gil was irritated by Pete's words. He started to shift his anger to Pete, but Rafe intervened.

"Come on, boy, it wasn't Pete's fault. We're ready for lunch. How about a ham sandwich all around?"

The other two agreed, and Rafe started a production line that hurried up the process, giving directions to Gil and Pete.

When they were seated at the table, Gil said, "I have to thank you, Rafe. You were right about what was wrong. She'd already intended to cut back her work hours a little. And Kelly and Mary made it easy for her. She'll change places with Mary during Drew's naps or when he's playing. She'll go upstairs and lie down on the couch. And they're going to hire a schoolgirl to work part-time, so she doesn't feel guilty leaving Kelly to close every day.''

"How late do they stay open?'' Pete asked, suddenly wondering if Kelly was going to be in danger. He'd thought both women had been there every night.

"Usually at six, but on Monday and Thursday night, they stay open until nine.''

Pete stared into space. Maybe he could go to the store on those nights and hang around, be sure everything was all right. He'd planned on dropping in on Tuesday night, but he could change that to tonight. And he'd be there on Thursday to go to the doctor's appointment. Maybe he could stay in town and come back later. Or spend the day with Drew. The little guy was okay. He was surprised how much he liked him.

"That's good for Lindsay, but Mary or Kelly will have to do the late closings. That's tough,'' Rafe complained.

"Yeah,'' Pete agreed.

Gil answered with a voice of steel, "But Lindsay's pregnant.''

"Maybe Pete and I can take turns going to town those nights,'' Rafe said, frowning. "We could make sure everything goes okay.''

Gil grinned. "Then you can have the fight that I had yesterday evening. It's a safe neighborhood. I'm sure everything will be all right.''

Pete knew he'd find out Kelly's attitude tonight when he showed up. Maybe he'd better think of something to shop for. Would Kelly know his mother's birthday?

Probably not. He'd say he was looking for a present for his mom.

And he'd be very picky.

Right up until closing time.

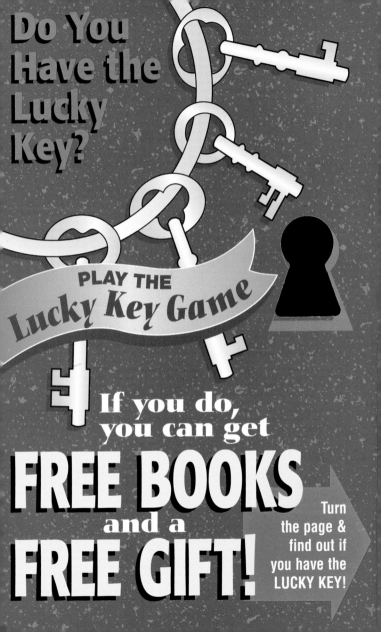

PLAY THE
Lucky Key Game
and get

HOW TO PLAY:

1. With a coin, carefully scratch off gold area at the right. Then check the claim chart to see what we have for you — **2 FREE BOOKS** and a **FREE GIFT** — **ALL YOURS FREE!**

2. Send back the card and you'll receive two brand-new Silhouette Romance® books. These books have a cover price of $3.99 each in the U.S. and $4.50 each in Canada, but they are yours to keep absolutely free.

3. There's no catch. You're under no obligation to buy anything. We charge nothing —ZERO — for your first shipment. And you don't have to make any minimum number of purchases — not even one!

4. The fact is, thousands of readers enjoy receiving books by mail from the Silhouette Reader Service™. They enjoy the convenience of home delivery...they like getting the best new novels at discount prices, **BEFORE** they're available in stores...and they love their *Heart to Heart* subscriber newsletter featuring author news, horoscopes, recipes, book reviews and much more!

5. We hope that after receiving your free books you'll want to remain a subscriber. But the choice is yours — to continue or cancel, any time at all! So why not take us up on our invitation, with no risk of any kind. You'll be glad you did!

YOURS FREE!
A SURPRISE GIFT

We can't tell you what it is...but we're sure you'll like it! A
FREE GIFT—
just for playing the LUCKY KEY game!

Visit us online at
www.eHarlequin.com

FREE GIFTS!

NO COST! NO OBLIGATION TO BUY!
NO PURCHASE NECESSARY!

PLAY THE
Lucky Key Game

Scratch gold area with a coin.
Then check below to see the books and gift you get!

315 SDL DH24
215 SDL DH2Y

YES! I have scratched off the gold area. Please send me the 2 Free books and gift for which I qualify. I understand I am under no obligation to purchase any books, as explained on the back and on the opposite page.

NAME   (PLEASE PRINT CLEARLY)

ADDRESS

APT.#   CITY

STATE/PROV.   ZIP/POSTAL CODE

2 free books plus a gift		1 free book
2 free books		Try Again!

(S-R-OS-02/02)

The Silhouette Reader Service™ — Here's how it works:

Accepting your 2 free books and gift places you under no obligation to buy anything. You may keep the books and gift and return the shipping statement marked "cancel." If you do not cancel, about a month later we'll send you 6 additional books and bill you just $3.15 each in the U.S., or $3.50 each in Canada, plus 25¢ shipping & handling per book and applicable taxes if any.* That's the complete price and — compared to cover prices of $3.99 each in the U.S. and $4.50 each in Canada — it's quite a bargain! You may cancel at any time, but if you choose to continue, every month we'll send you 6 more books, which you may either purchase at the discount price or return to us and cancel your subscription.

*Terms and prices subject to change without notice. Sales tax applicable in N.Y. Canadian residents will be charged applicable provincial taxes and GST.

If offer card is missing write to: Silhouette Reader Service, 3010 Walden Ave., P.O. Box 1867, Buffalo, NY 14240-1867

BUSINESS REPLY MAIL
FIRST-CLASS MAIL   PERMIT NO. 717-003   BUFFALO, NY

POSTAGE WILL BE PAID BY ADDRESSEE

SILHOUETTE READER SERVICE
3010 WALDEN AVE
PO BOX 1867
BUFFALO NY 14240-9952

NO POSTAGE
NECESSARY
IF MAILED
IN THE
UNITED STATES

Chapter Seven

Lindsay stayed until two o'clock, as she'd promised, because Kelly sent her up for lunch and a half hour's break about eleven-thirty. Then Lindsay and Mary took over the store while Kelly had lunch and did some housework until Drew went down for a late nap.

She came back to the store and sent Mary back to the apartment. "And it's time for you to go home and have your nap," she told Lindsay.

"But that leaves you on your own until closing, and it's a late night," Lindsay protested.

"I've worked late a lot of times. And Mom's upstairs if I get desperate. I'll be fine." After a little more convincing, she watched Lindsay leave. Her friend needed a nap during the early part of her pregnancy. Later on, she'd have trouble sleeping.

The store wasn't terribly busy in the afternoons until

school got out, so Kelly got a lot of work done, in particular tagging an order of dresses that came in.

Normally her mother would come down and relieve her for dinner for half an hour, but as soon as school was out, two high school girls applied for a part-time job.

"How did you hear we were looking for someone?" Kelly asked.

"Betty Sue's my cousin," the shorter of the two girls responded. "And I told Sue," she added gesturing to her friend.

Kelly asked them several questions. Then she decided to hire both of them on a trial basis. "I think we'll be able to use both of you, on different days. Mondays and Thursdays, we'll want you from four to eight. The other days from four to six-thirty. And all day Saturday. Would that be possible?"

"Both of us?" Sally, Betty Sue's cousin, asked.

"No. We'll split the weekdays. We might want both of you on Saturdays."

Both girls nodded eagerly.

"All right. We'll need your parents' okay. Let me write up something for you to get signed. When will you be able to start?"

"Today?" They both said at once.

"But we have to get these papers signed," Kelly said.

"My mom's waiting in the car outside," Sally said.

"I'll call my mom and she'll come sign it," Sue added.

Kelly chuckled quietly. "I hope you keep your enthusiasm. Okay, Sally, ask your mom to come in, and Sue, call yours.'' As she finished, the shop door jangled and Kelly went to wait on a customer.

When she completed the sale, she had Sally's mom waiting. She hurriedly wrote up the terms of employment. By the time she'd done that, Sue's mother had arrived also. Suddenly she and Lindsay had two employees, at least for a month.

She allowed the girls to handle the next few customers that came in. The only difficulty she ran across was the girls wanting to talk to their friends. But a quiet word to each of them cured that problem. Kelly spent her time catching up on paperwork and keeping an eye on the girls, but she found life much easier.

Business usually died down around six and picked up again around seven on Monday and Thursday nights. After having called her mother, asking her to fix dinner for the two girls, Kelly sent them upstairs at six. She didn't want to leave either girl downstairs on her own just yet.

Shortly after she rejoined the girls after dinner and business was picking up, the bell over the door jangled again. And Pete Crawford walked in.

Sue, tossing her blond hair over her shoulder, hurried up to him, batting her eyelashes.

Kelly made a mental note to remind Sue not to flirt with men customers. Wives and girlfriends wouldn't appreciate that behavior. Not that it bothered her, and Pete, of course, didn't have a steady girlfriend.

Kelly moved to Sue's side. "Good evening, Pete. Can we help you with anything?"

"I offered," Sue hurriedly said.

"Good. Could you clear the last dressing room? I think there are a lot of clothes in there." Though Kelly smiled at Sue, she made sure the girl knew she wasn't giving her a choice.

"I didn't know you had part-time help. Sue was just telling me it's her first day."

"Yes, she and Sally came in today. With Lindsay pregnant, it seemed like a good idea to hire them."

"Yeah. So you'll have someone with you until closing?"

"No, I don't want to keep the girls out that late on a school night. They'll go home at eight."

Pete frowned.

"Why does that bother you?" she asked.

"I don't think it's good for you to be here alone until nine o'clock," he protested.

"This is not a high-crime district, Pete. I'll be fine." Though his behavior irritated her, it left a warm spot in her tummy, too. Her husband never concerned himself with her safety or happiness. But Pete seemed to worry about her. Not that she needed his help, but it did make her feel good.

They stood there for a minute and she did a quick visual check on the girls. They seemed to be okay, except Sue did shoot her an aggrieved look.

"Was there something you were looking for?"

"Uh, yeah. It's my mom's birthday. I thought I'd see

what you have for her. But first, I wondered if I could go see Drew before his bedtime.''

''I don't mind, but he goes down fairly early. Let me call Mom and see if he's still awake.'' Kelly really didn't want him going upstairs to see Drew. She didn't want her son to become friends with Pete. He wouldn't be around all that often. Drew would be upset when he stopped visiting.

Mary seemed delighted that Pete was there and invited him up at once. ''He can visit with Rafe.''

''Rafe's there? I didn't realize—okay, sure, I'll send Pete up.'' She hung up the phone and turned to Pete. ''Rafe's there. Mom said come on up.''

She noticed that Pete didn't show any surprise about Rafe's visit. ''Did you know he was coming?''

''Nope. He didn't say he was.''

She shrugged her shoulders. ''Okay. Just go knock on the door.''

She stood behind the counter and watched his long legs eat up the stairs.

''He's a hottie, isn't he?'' Sue said wistfully.

''Yes, he is, but, Sue, don't flirt with the men who come in. It alienates the women in their lives. I expect you to act professional.''

The girl's cheeks turned rosy. ''If you're jealous of me—'' she began.

Kelly should have expected that response since the rumors in town said she and Pete were a couple. She stared at the young woman. Then, drawing a deep breath, she said, ''I'm talking about the behavior we expect from anyone representing our store. If you find it too difficult, we can end our association immediately.''

Sue turned on her heel and huffed her way to the latest customer to enter the store. Kelly watched her until she was sure she was graciously waiting on the customer. Then she turned back to her work.

Damn Pete Crawford. It had never occurred to her that he could create a problem in their store. But trouble seemed to follow him wherever he went.

Mary offered Pete a cup of coffee. He accepted gratefully. With Drew on his knee, he leaned to Rafe. "Sorry I didn't let you know I'd check on them tonight. We should take turns so it won't be so obvious what we're doing."

Casually Rafe shrugged his shoulders, his gaze on Mary. "I explained to Mary."

Pete exclaimed, "You what?"

Drew grabbed Pete's shirt, as if afraid he was about to be dumped, and Pete calmed himself. "Sorry, little guy. I didn't mean to startle you." He hugged the little boy close and Drew reached up to pat his cheek lovingly.

"Is something wrong?" Mary asked as she came toward them, carrying Pete's cup of coffee and a plate of cookies in her other hand.

"No, of course not," Pete said.

Rafe also reassured her. "I told him you knew why we were both here tonight."

"It's so sweet of you, Pete, to worry about Kelly."

Pete didn't think that would be Kelly's reaction. "Uh, it might be best not to mention that to Kelly."

"Probably not," Mary agreed. She put down the plate of cookies. "Drew and I made these cookies this afternoon, didn't we, Drew? Would you like to give one to Pete?"

Obviously Drew understood his grandmother because he wiggled closer to the plate and scooped up a cookie and tried to put it in Pete's mouth.

Pete took it from him and took a bite. "Mmm-mmm, good." Then he pretended to bite Drew, too, which had the boy squealing with glee.

"You two get along so well," Mary said with a smile. Then she gasped and added, "I didn't mean anything by that, Pete, truly."

He felt guilty at Mary's reaction. "I didn't even think that, Mary, I promise. But it's easy to get along with Drew. He doesn't say much I can disagree with," he said with a grin.

"He doesn't talk a lot, but lately he's talking more," Mary assured him, in a protective manner. "He's very bright."

"Of course he is," Pete agreed. "I think he's getting sleepy. Why don't I bathe him and then read him a story. It will give you and Rafe some time to visit."

He didn't think he'd draw any objection from Rafe, but Mary frowned. "Are you sure? He splashes at lot when he bathes."

"I know. I bathed him Saturday night."

"Oh! I didn't realize—well, then that would be nice."

Pete took the little boy to his bedroom. After he undressed Drew, he took off his own shirt. He didn't want to go back down to the store looking like he'd gone for a swim.

They played in the bathroom for about ten minutes and he found the little boy easy to understand. Then, just as he was ready to end the bath, the door opened and Kelly stood there staring at his bare chest.

"What—what are you doing?" she gasped.

"Finishing up Drew's bath. I volunteered to take care of him to give Mary and Rafe some time alone." He knew Kelly would be in favor of that maneuver. He lifted a giggling Drew from the bath and wrapped him in a bath towel.

"But—but your shirt," she protested, her gaze fixed on his chest.

He liked her looking at him. He'd like to look at her, but they were only pretending. He kept reminding himself of that as her chest heaved.

She reached out for Drew and the boy extended his arms to his mother.

"You'll get wet," Pete reminded her. "Let me dry him off first."

"I don't have time. The girls leave in five minutes. I'll just kiss him good-night." Leaving Drew in Pete's arms, she leaned over and kissed her child. Pete wanted to put his arms around her, to pull her closer for his kiss, too. But they were pretending.

"Are you busy downstairs?" he hurriedly asked as she turned toward the door.

"Not too busy. Why?"

"I need a lot of help choosing something for Mom."

"I think I can manage to help you. I've got to go."

After the door closed behind her, Pete dressed Drew in his pajamas, talking to the little boy all the while. "Your mama is pretty good, isn't she? You're a lucky little boy. Not only that, Drew, she's beautiful. I know that doesn't matter to you, but it sure does catch a man's eye."

Drew put a little finger beside his eye. "Eye!"

"Way to go, guy! That's exactly right. Where's your nose?"

He was delighted when Drew touched Pete's nose.

"Close enough. Okay, let's get you in bed now and I'll read a story to you." He felt guilty when he checked out the storybooks and found a short one. But he wanted to get downstairs with Kelly. For her protection, of course. Nothing else.

Drew struggled to stay awake, but his eyes drifted shut before the third page. Pete waited until he was sure the boy was asleep before he got up. He thought there was nothing sweeter than a little one asleep. That thought surprised him. He'd never even seen a child asleep close-up before.

When he came out of Drew's bedroom, Rafe yanked his arm from the back of the couch and Mary, beside him, blushed.

Pete said quickly, "I'm going downstairs to shop. See you guys later."

They both said good-night, but Pete figured they were

glad he was gone. If it had been him on the sofa with Kelly, he would've been. Except that he'd promised himself he wouldn't touch her unless it was for the pretense.

Damn.

There were several women still shopping. The two teenagers were gone. Only Kelly was there to handle the customers. The front door opened again and several groups of women entered. Suddenly Kelly had more than she could handle. Pete moved to the cash register to ring up sales.

"Do you want me to call Mary?" he quietly asked Kelly.

Since the door opened again, Kelly nodded.

Pete pressed the intercom. "Mary, we need you."

Rafe came down with her. "Anything I can do?"

Pete drafted him. "Yeah. Fold and put their purchases in a bag as I ring them up."

Pete figured the rush would dissipate soon, but it didn't. The store remained full until nine o'clock. Several customers lingered even beyond closing time.

When they finally left, carrying their packages, Pete leaned his elbows on the counter. "Wow, you did a lot of business tonight."

"Yes, we did," Kelly said, smiling, but exhaustion was evident in her face. "I think word got around that we received some new shipments."

"You two were wonderful," Mary added. "We wouldn't have done nearly as well if you hadn't been here."

"That's true," Kelly agreed. "I'll be glad to pay you—"

"Don't even think of it. I owe you," Pete said.

"Mary can repay me by going to the movies with me on Friday night," Rafe said, staring at Mary.

Her answer was a beaming smile. "I'd love to. Oh, I—I might need to take care of Drew."

"No, Mom. Drew will be with me," Kelly said quietly.

"Yeah, we'll take him to the fair that's coming to town. He'll love it." Pete could tell his words surprised Kelly, but he knew she wouldn't want to leave Drew with anyone.

Suddenly Kelly looked up. "You didn't get to find a present for your mother, Pete. Do you want to look now?"

"No, we're all too tired tonight. I have a little while before her birthday. Maybe I'll come in on Thursday." She wouldn't question him coming in with that excuse. He knew she'd catch on eventually, but the longer she didn't the better.

"Well," Kelly began, walking to the door, "I'm sure you're ready to head home."

Rafe hurriedly said, "I left my hat upstairs. I'll go up and get it and go out the upstairs exit. Mary can let me out."

The older couple turned and headed upstairs.

Pete looked at Kelly. "Are you going to be able to manage until Lindsay has her baby?"

"Of course. Since Drew goes down so early, we can

use the baby monitor and Mom can come down and help. But I do appreciate your help tonight.''

She opened the door and held it open, waiting for him to leave.

He was reluctant to go. "I'll be back on Thursday morning to take you to the doctor, but I think Drew has completely recovered.''

"He's doing well.''

"So you don't think the fair will be too much for him on Friday night?'' He wanted to get a commitment now.

"You'd probably have more fun if you went with someone else. He won't last all that long.''

Pete shook his head. "I don't, either. But a corn dog or two and maybe some cotton candy would be fun. Has Drew ever had cotton candy?''

"Absolutely not. It's not good for a child.''

"Aw, come on, Kelly. A little bit wouldn't hurt. You can't handicap him like that. He'll be teased in school if he goes without having had cotton candy.'' He was enchanted by the smile she gave him.

"Maybe just a little. I wouldn't want him to be teased.''

"All right!'' he enthused and held up a hand for a high five.

Her reluctant smile broadened a little as she reached up.

"I told him tonight he has a great mom.''

"I doubt he understood,'' she pointed out.

"He did. We're communicating well.''

"Pete—don't get too friendly with Drew. When this is over, he won't understand. He'll miss you."

Pete stared at Kelly. He hadn't thought about the end of their pretense. "Hey, maybe we won't stop pretending. It might be a good idea to continue. Neither of us wants to marry, so we could keep company and not hurt anyone else."

"No, I don't think so."

"But Kelly—"

"It's late, Pete. Time for you to go."

He noticed the traffic picking up a little. "Okay, but we should try to convince everyone right away, then. So I'm going to kiss you good-night while the cars are going by."

Without waiting for her agreement, Pete slid his arms around her tempting body and pulled her against him. Then his lips covered hers. This kiss wasn't a brush of lips, a brief salute. No, this time his tongue invaded her mouth and he held her against him, committing every inch of his body to her. He almost cheered when her arms slowly climbed his chest to wrap themselves around his neck. But he was afraid if he took his mouth away, she might remember she didn't like him to touch her.

He reslanted his lips over hers, loving the touch and feel of her, the sweet scent of her. He risked breaking off the kiss to taste the soft skin behind her ear. When she didn't pull away, he nibbled on her neck, wishing he could explore lower. Then she started pulling back and his lips returned to hers. He wasn't ready to let her go.

"Pete!" she gasped, pulling her mouth from his. "Surely that's enough."

He kissed her again, as if he hadn't understood. She pulled away again. "Pete, please."

He couldn't ignore her plea. She sounded stressed. Of course he was going to be stressed when he left. So stressed he'd need a cold shower.

"Uh, I think someone's watching us," he muttered and ran his hands up and back down her back. "I think I need to kiss you again." He lowered his lips again, but she buried her face in his shirt.

"No, that's enough." Putting her hands on his chest, she shoved him away.

He could've held on. He was a lot stronger than her, but he didn't want to scare her. Or eliminate the possibility of ever kissing her again. She was a top-notch kisser. And if Rafe's story about her husband was true, the man had also been an idiot.

"Okay," he muttered, not kissing her, just holding her against him.

"You'd better go."

"I will as soon as you kiss me goodbye."

Kelly stared at him as if he'd lost his mind. "What do you think we were just doing?"

"I was enjoying myself. I hope you were, too."

"Go home, Pete," she ordered sternly.

With a grimace, he brushed her lips with his, one of those casual kisses, and did as she'd commanded. But he didn't want to.

Chapter Eight

On Tuesday morning, Pete's behavior caught up with him.

As he swung into the saddle, one of his brothers, Rick, said in falsetto, "Pete, can you get me another size. This dress is too tight."

He ignored his brother's teasing, but Mike and Joe, his other brothers working on the ranch, didn't.

"What are you talking about?" Joe, the oldest, demanded.

"Haven't you heard?" Rick asked. "Our brother has been selling dresses in Lindsay and Kelly's store."

All three men stared at Pete. He was suddenly glad his fourth brother, Logan, lived in Texas and couldn't tease him. At least not today.

"Cut it out. I was working the cash register so Lindsay could get some rest. She's pregnant, you know.'' He figured they wouldn't tease him about helping Lindsay.

"I heard it wasn't Lindsay you were with, but Kelly. You've taken her out once or twice even. I didn't think she dated.''

Pete decided Rick was listening too closely to gossip. "I took her out once...so far. It's no big deal.''

Joe looked from Rick to Pete. "I heard you were dating Sheila Hooten.''

Rick grinned. "You're behind on the gossip, big bro. He dumped Sheila. She's trying to hang on, but my money's on Pete.''

"What do you mean, trying to hang on? What's she doing?'' Mike asked, already in the saddle.

"She's telling everyone Pete proposed and they're going to be married. But with Pete hanging out with Kelly, everyone's wondering.''

"You boys have nothing to do but gossip?'' Caleb Crawford said to his sons. He'd just come to the barn, as far as they knew. Pete hoped that was true.

"No, sir,'' all four responded and headed for the north pasture. They were cutting out the cows soon to be new mamas.

Pete didn't keep up with his brothers. When his father rode alongside him, he said, "Dad, uh, I need to talk to you.''

"Yeah?'' Caleb said, easing back on the reins.

"I need Thursday off. I'm going to take Kelly and Drew to his doctor appointment.''

"She needs help?''

Pete avoided his father's gaze. "Uh, yeah, it's hard to manage by herself."

"So it's true?"

"What's true?"

"You're serious about Kelly?"

Pete almost fell off his horse. He swallowed and carefully said, "No, of course not. You know I don't intend to marry. But—but we're friends. I don't mind offering a helping hand. She's having to do a lot more since Lindsay got pregnant."

"Okay. I think we can manage without you," Caleb agreed, but he reminded himself to discuss the situation with his wife Carol. She was better at knowing what was going on with their children.

"We did a lot of business last night," Kelly reported to Lindsay when she arrived the next morning.

"That's good but how did you manage?"

"Well, until eight o'clock, I had two teenagers working for us. Sally and Sue came in after school yesterday and wanted a job. I took them on a temporary basis for a month. They'll each work four to six-thirty two days a week, four to eight one day, and all day Saturday."

"Wow, that was fast. Were they good?" Lindsay was sitting at the kitchen table having a cup of hot tea since the doctor limited her to one cup of coffee a day.

"Yes, with a few corrections. The only real problem was Sue flirting with customers. Pete came in last night."

"But he was here yesterday morning, wasn't he? Why did he come back last night?"

"To buy your mother a birthday present. And a good thing he did. He and Rafe handled the cash register and bagging purchases. That helped a lot."

Lindsay was frowning, but before she could speak, someone knocked on the outside door. Kelly opened the door to find Carol Crawford, Lindsay's mother, standing there. "Come in, Mrs. Crawford."

"You know I said for you to call me Carol, Kelly. We're all adults, now."

"Yes, Carol, I will. Come have a cup of tea."

"Thank you. I'd love one."

Mary entered the kitchen at that moment and greeted Carol, too, as she joined them at the table.

"I hear you're having a birthday soon," Mary said. "Happy birthday, whenever it is."

Carol looked at her strangely. "Thank you, Mary."

"Her birthday is in October," Lindsay said. "Don't you think it's a little early for shopping?"

"October?" Kelly questioned. "But Pete said—I mean, I must've misunderstood him." Kelly busied herself making Mary a cup of tea.

"Not likely. Pete was using it as an excuse to visit," Lindsay said. "You said Rafe was here, too, on the same night? Did they plan it?" Lindsay asked, but Kelly thought it was a rhetorical question.

Mary, however, had an answer. "Actually, if they'd planned it, they wouldn't have both shown up on the same night."

"Mom, what are you talking about?"

Mary turned to her daughter. "Rafe told me. They were both worried about you closing at nine o'clock by yourself and they wanted to protect you."

Kelly stared at her mother, trying to decide how to react. It was nice that Pete was concerned about her. Though he probably was afraid he'd have to find another woman who didn't want to marry. But she could take care of herself. And she'd tell him so!

"Good," Lindsay said. "I was worried about that, too."

"Lindsay, you of all people should know I can take care of myself. I'm a mother, remember?"

Carol chimed in. "And a very good one, I must say, Kelly, but that doesn't mean you shouldn't be careful. I'm glad Pete is being cautious." Her smile widened even more. "And I applaud his taste in women."

Kelly covered her face with her hands. Then she looked at her friend. "Tell her, Lindsay."

"Tell me what?" Carol asked.

"Mom, uh, Kelly's helping Pete get out of the clutches of Sheila Hooten. She's pretending to be his girlfriend," Lindsay said. Much to Kelly's surprise, she added, "Of course, I'd like for it to be true."

"So would I," Carol agreed. "I worry about Pete. He was engaged once and found out the woman only wanted him for the money he has. He thought she was his one true love. He hasn't been willing to risk his heart since."

"Oh," Kelly said softly. "I think that's Sheila's reason, too. She's not very nice."

"I know. Believe me, we're grateful for any help you can give us. We'd all be miserable if he married her."

"Actually I think they've almost convinced everyone," Lindsay said. "I've heard Sheila is telling everyone Pete asked her to marry him, but since he's dating Kelly, everyone is questioning her words."

"And I hear someone else is hanging around the place, too," Carol added, looking at Mary.

Kelly wanted to say that was the only good thing to come out of their pretense, but she couldn't say that in front of Pete's mother. "Rafe and Mom are going to the movies on Friday night."

"I can baby-sit Drew if you and Pete want to join them," Carol suggested.

"No, thank you."

"Pete's taking Drew and Kelly to the fair that's setting up on the edge of town," Mary said, looking quite pleased with their future plans.

Kelly didn't add anything to the conversation. She still wasn't sure it would be a good thing to do. But she did have a little more sympathy for Pete. A broken heart was a painful thing.

"Carol, you didn't say why you stopped by. Is everything all right?" Kelly asked to fill the awkward silence.

"Oh, yes. I wanted to check on Lindsay without pestering Gil. I thought I'd stop by here before I went to the hospital board meeting this morning."

"Why don't you two visit then, while Mom and I go downstairs and set things up. Drew is playing in his room but he likes to watch *Sesame Street* at ten o'clock.''

"I don't mean to run you off, Kelly. Really.''

"No problem. I didn't straighten the store last night. I was too tired, so I have to clean up. I'm glad we got a chance to visit, though. Come by any time,'' Kelly said.

Mary followed Kelly downstairs. "She's such a nice lady.''

"Yes, she is.''

"She'd make a wonderful mother-in-law,'' Mary added.

Kelly spun around on the stairs. "Mom! Remember it's pretense! Pete doesn't want to marry anyone. And he doesn't want to be a father.''

"But he bathed Drew last night. He seems to like him. He said he did when I complimented him on—'' Mary broke off, looking guilty.

"Mother, you didn't try to talk him into being a father again, did you?''

"No. And I apologized at once, but he said he wasn't upset.''

Kelly's shoulders sagged. Life seemed so complicated lately.

"Is there any hope?'' Carol asked her daughter.

"I don't know. I have my fingers crossed. Something happened the first date. It didn't go well, though I'm not sure why. But Pete was very supportive at the hospital.

He's been wonderful, Mom. I admit I didn't think he had it in him, but I was wrong."

Carol smiled. "He's a good man, Lindsay. I think he's afraid of getting hurt again. But it would be so wonderful if he and Kelly…" She sighed, staring into space, imagining a happy, settled future for her son. "I really don't understand why only one of our sons has married."

"You're wanting more grandchildren," Lindsay accused her mother. "I'm working on it as fast as I can."

"I know you are, darling," Carol responded, patting her hand. "But Logan's babies are in Texas. I know it's not that far, but too far for daily, even weekly, contact."

"We'll have to be patient, Mom. I don't want Kelly unhappy, either. She's already had her heart broken, too. I guess she and Pete have a lot in common after all."

"Yes, they do. Kelly is a sweetheart."

"It's a good thing Sheila is so stubborn," Lindsay said with a grin. "Pete would hate me if he heard me say it, but I'm afraid if Sheila went away, he wouldn't see Kelly anymore. As long as Sheila's there, Kelly and Pete will be together."

"Should I send Sheila a thank-you note?" Carol asked with a smile.

"No. We don't want to let her know that we appreciate her. She might think she's winning."

"True. Well, let me know if I can help."

"I wondered if maybe it might be a good idea to invite Kelly and Mary and Drew to Sunday dinner. Pete's never brought a lady to Sunday dinner."

"Oh, good thinking. Will Pete cooperate?"

"I think so. He's taking Kelly and Drew to the doctor on Thursday. He's becoming attached to Drew."

"Even better. Okay, I'll ask him about picking up Mary, Kelly and Drew on Sunday after church. That's a great idea, darling. Is there anything special you want me to cook?"

"Mmm, I'm craving strawberry shortcake. Is that okay?"

"It's your father's favorite, too. I'll make several so everyone will have plenty."

"And I can take the leftovers home!" Lindsay added with a grin.

"Right, as a reward for your brilliant idea." Carol stood and leaned over to kiss her daughter's cheek. "I've got to go now for my meeting, but I'll see you Sunday if not before."

Lindsay walked her mother to the door and watched her go down the stairs and get into her car. Lindsay hoped she was doing the right thing, pushing Kelly and Pete together. She wanted them both to be happy.

Pete was worried.

He loved his work. He'd never been someone who liked to dress in suits and ties, work indoors, even on the most bitterly cold day.

He was a cowboy, through and through.

But excitement was filling him because on Thursday, instead of going out and chasing cows, he was going to see Kelly and Drew. What was wrong with him?

Even the best sex hadn't done that to him. And he

wasn't getting any sex with Kelly. He thought about those kisses on Monday night. They'd been memorable, he'd admit. But they hadn't been real. They'd both known they were pretending.

Maybe he was looking forward to Thursday because he liked helping Kelly. Sure, that could be it. Kelly was a friend who was—who needed help.

He tried to think of something else, anything else, before he could examine that statement too closely. Because lurking under that inane excuse was the fact that he wanted Kelly. And not for her conversational skills.

As penance for not working Thursday morning, Pete put in a couple of hours on Wednesday doing paperwork, both for his father and himself. He was running his own herd in with his father's. He'd bought some land alongside his father's, but his cows were run in with his father's, and they both used his pastures, too.

On Thursday morning he dressed in a sport shirt and slacks, so the doctor wouldn't show him up. He didn't like the interest the man took in Kelly.

When he got to Kelly's, he thought she looked a little dressed up to him. She and her mother were both in the store, with Drew playing with his blocks on the bottom two steps of the stairway.

"Good morning," he said with a friendly smile.

Both women greeted him.

"You're real dressed up, Kelly. Are we going in to Oklahoma City for this appointment?" he asked, liking the knit dress she wore because it definitely outlined her curves. But he didn't want to think she wore it for the doctor's sake.

"I'm glad you like the dress, Pete. It's one of our new ones. But the appointment is here in Lawton. It shouldn't take long."

"Good. I'll take us to lunch afterward as a reward. How about that, Drew? Want to go eat after we see the doctor?"

Drew, who had stopped playing with his blocks when he heard Pete's voice, popped to his feet and came toddling over with a big smile.

Pete swept him into the air, with Drew squealing, before bringing him down into his arms. Drew hugged his neck.

"Be careful," Kelly urged hurriedly. "He'll drool on you."

"No problem," Pete told her, pulling out a clean handkerchief to wipe the little boy's mouth.

"A man with a handkerchief," Mary exclaimed. "I love that!"

"I'll be sure and tell Rafe," Pete teased.

Mary laughed, but her cheeks turned bright pink. Since a customer entered, she turned her attention to the newcomer, leaving Pete and Kelly alone.

"Looks like things are going well for Mary and Rafe," he whispered, as he bent over to put Drew down.

"I hope so. Are you ready?"

"Yeah, but we've got plenty of time. Are you that anxious to see the doc?"

She turned to stare at him. "I'll be glad to know Drew's okay."

"Come on, Kelly. You know what I mean."

"No, I don't," she said, frowning.

"You dress extra special nice and you're anxious to get there early. Anyone could figure that out." He ran his gaze over her formfitting dress. "*And* you're dressed sexy. You sure didn't dress like this when we went to the movies."

"Are you insinuating—" she broke off, her mouth hanging open. Then she lifted her hand.

He grabbed it. "You've already slapped me once, Kelly. I don't think we want to go down that road again. At least, I know I don't."

"Get out, Pete. I don't need your help. And I'm not flirting with the doctor. I'm the one who doesn't want to marry, remember?" Her voice was tight with anger.

"I don't know. I've heard doctors are pretty tempting. After all, they don't have money problems."

"You've been hanging out with the wrong kind of women," she replied.

Her barb struck home. The woman he'd believed he loved, ten years ago, had set her sights on him because of his family's money. He'd been heartbroken. Without thinking, he wanted Kelly to feel his pain. "I've yet to find any woman who doesn't have a calculator for a heart."

"Well, the men I've known aren't any better," she returned.

"Your husband married you for your money?" He knew that couldn't be true.

"No. He married me because he had to, and then pretended he wasn't married. He had more girlfriends in the six months we were married than I had fingers. It wasn't pleasant."

Drew, who had returned to his blocks when the adults began talking, looked up at his mother with a frown, as if he sensed a problem. "Mama?"

"Yes, baby. Everything's fine," she told her son, bending down to scoop him into her arms. She tried to walk past Pete.

Pete grabbed her arm. "Where are you going?"

"To the doctor's office. Let me go."

"Like hell I will. You promised I could go with you so everyone would believe we were serious."

"Surely you don't expect me to continue after your insinuations?"

"Why not? Unless they're true." He stared at her, a challenge in his gaze.

"It doesn't matter whether they're true or not. You've insulted me. I can't be expected to continue with our charade."

Okay, so he'd gone too far. But he was fighting for his woman— No! No. He was fighting for his reputation. That's what he was fighting for. "You promised."

"Really, Pete—"

"Aren't you two going? You don't want to be late," Mary said after the customer left.

"She wasn't interested in anything?" Kelly asked, rather than answering her mother's question.

"Not today, but she wants a dress like yours. She's coming back tonight with her husband. That was a good idea of Lindsay's for you to wear that knit dress out. It's going to be good advertising."

So Kelly hadn't chosen that dress for the doctor, Pete realized. It was advertising for the store. Most men he knew would vote to see their women in that dress if it did for them what it did for Kelly.

Kelly didn't look at him at all. She again began to leave. He kept hold of her arm, but moved with her to the door.

"I don't want you to go with us," she muttered, hoping obviously that her mother wouldn't hear her.

"You promised," he reminded her again. "Besides, your mom explained why you're dressed like that."

"My dress has nothing to do with you."

"Look, I know we're pretending, but it hurts a guy's ego to think his date is dressing for another man."

"But I did dress for another man, Mr. Crawford. Just not the doctor." Then she walked out the door.

Pete hurried after her.

Chapter Nine

Pete didn't get to ask any questions about that elusive man who had inspired Kelly's wardrobe. Well, that wasn't quite correct. He'd asked. She'd refused to answer.

She still wasn't speaking to him when they returned to the store an hour later. Her mother was waiting on a customer and Lindsay sat on a stool behind the counter.

"What did the doctor say about Drew?" she asked at once.

"He's fine," Kelly said.

"Aha! She speaks!" Pete announced in a disgruntled voice.

Lindsay looked from one to the other. Then she asked, "Okay, what's wrong?"

Kelly didn't answer.

Pete, however, was glad to have someone respond.

"She thinks I insulted her because I asked if she wore that sexy dress for the doctor."

Lindsay beamed. "It is sexy, isn't it? On a hanger, it looks like nothing. That's why I suggested Kelly wear it."

"Yeah, it's sexy. But I didn't know why she was wearing it," he said, his voice filled with justification.

Lindsay stared at him, and Pete got worried when her eyes lit up with joy. "Pete, you're jealous!"

"Don't be ridiculous!" he shouted, drawing the attention of several of the women shopping.

Kelly stepped into the conversation she'd been trying to ignore. "Lindsay, you're wrong. Pete thinks everything a woman does has to do with the—let's see, what was it Pete?—the calculator in her heart. And he's so right. I wore this dress to sell more of them so I'll have more money for my man."

Pete noted the surprise on Lindsay's face. Guess she didn't know this mystery man, either. No help there. "Who is he?"

"I believe you asked that before."

"Yeah, and you didn't answer me."

"It's none of your business!" she snapped and headed for the stairs. "I'm putting Drew down for his nap. Then I'll be back down."

Pete stood there, his hands on his hips, staring at her as she went up the stairs. Yeah, that dress was definitely sexy. On Kelly.

A lady tapped him on the shoulder. "Sir, do you think

my husband would look at me like that if I bought that dress?''

Surprised, he stared at the forty-year-old woman, her figure round. Lindsay sent him a warning look, but he wouldn't hurt the woman's feelings. ''Couldn't hurt,'' he said with a smile.

The customer beamed at him. ''You're right.''

''You might try that royal-blue. That would look good on you with those pretty blue eyes of yours,'' he added.

She slapped his arm and giggled. ''It's not my eyes I want him to notice!''

''Yes, ma'am,'' he acknowledged with a grin.

Lindsay slipped her arm through his as the customer hurried over to Mary to ask to try on the knit dress.

''Well done, brother. She's happy.''

''I wish I had that effect on Kelly. And who do you think the man is?''

''Not the doctor?'' Lindsay asked.

''No. He's interested, but she'd barely talk to him. And I haven't seen anyone else around here.''

''There's no one else. The only man in her life is Drew,'' Lindsay said ruefully. Then she laughed. ''Oh, Pete, you idiot. She's referring to Drew.''

Pete gave her a hard stare. ''You mean she—'' He headed for the stairs.

''Pete, don't be too hard on her. You do seem to yank her chain.''

''Not half as much as she does mine!'' he informed his sister before he entered the apartment.

Lindsay whispered to herself. "I know…and it's wonderful!"

Kelly didn't know she'd been followed until the door to Drew's room opened. The boy had just lain down in his bed, but he popped up and squealed, "Pete!"

"Hey, buddy, that's the first time you ever said my name. Good boy!"

Kelly didn't think so. She didn't want her son to fall for Pete's charm. "He was just going to sleep!"

Pete leaned over the bed railing and hugged Drew. "He'll go to sleep, won't you, Drew? You need to get lots of sleep so you'll feel like going to the fair. We'll get cotton candy, and we'll ride some rides. You'll love it!"

Kelly knew her son had no idea what Pete had said because he'd never experienced cotton candy or rides. But the enthusiasm in Pete's voice made her think he was the Pied Piper.

"Lie down, Drew. When you wake up, you can watch *Sesame Street* again and have some cookies with Cookie Monster," she promised. She tried not to use food as bribery, but she couldn't get rid of Pete until she got Drew settled.

Drew flopped down on his pillow. "Night-night."

"Sleep tight," Kelly whispered, as she always did when he went to sleep, and dropped a kiss on the top of his head.

Then she tiptoed out of the room, knowing Pete would follow.

Without speaking to him, she grabbed the baby monitor, turned it on and slipped back into Drew's room. Maybe Pete would leave before she came out.

But he was still standing there, sexy, solid and determined.

"Why did you lie to me?"

"I didn't."

He took a step closer. "Yes, you did. Not an outright lie, but you led me to think there was someone else."

"There is!" she snapped.

"Yeah, Drew. Not exactly a lover."

"I never said he was my lover, but I love him."

"Of course you do. He's your child." He moved another step closer.

Kelly debated holding her ground, but Pete was getting a little too close for safety.

"I have to go back downstairs." She whirled around and headed for the door, but Pete circled her and leaned against the door, blocking her way.

"Not yet. I want to know why you misled me like that."

"To remind you that we're pretending. That my personal life has nothing to do with you. How could you forget?"

"I didn't forget," he ripped back.

She glared at him. "It seems to me you did." Without smiling she added, "Not that I think you were really jealous. You're a spoiled man. Women fawn over you and tell you anything you want to know. It's ridiculous!"

"I don't ask them to be so—so accommodating," he protested.

"I haven't seen you protesting. And you certainly don't like it when I don't kowtow to you," she pointed out. He couldn't argue with that.

"I'm concerned about convincing everyone. I'm a method actor, you know. That's why I'm so good at making our—our scheme look real."

Kelly gave him a disgusted look. "Please! I don't believe that."

"Well, you should. The only time you're believable is when I'm kissing you. Which means you need more practice."

Before she could protest, he pulled her against him and gave another sampling of his method acting.

Kelly wished she knew what to do to counteract the magic of his kisses. He was right. She kissed him as if he was her lover. She knew she did. But she didn't know how to stop. And she feared she still wouldn't have found an answer if he tried to take her to bed. A horrible, delicious thought.

He drew away before she could collect herself. "I'll see you tomorrow night about six." Then he moved her to one side, opened the door and ran down the steps.

What was she going to do? She'd promised herself she'd never let her hormones overrule her head. Once was enough. But Pete's touch was ten times more fascinating than James's.

He doesn't want a permanent relationship, remember? If you fall for him, you'll get your heart broken again. Even worse, Drew will, too. You've got to keep Drew safe.

She drew a deep breath, pushed back her hair, and went back to the store. "Are you tired, Lindsay?" she asked as soon as she got downstairs.

"No, I'm feeling pretty good. And Gil said he and Rafe would cook dinner tonight, so I'll stay an extra hour if you want to go rest."

"Thanks, but I'll let Mom go up." After Kelly sent her mother upstairs, she waited on a customer, straightened up some of the scarves on a table that had been messed up and finally, having nothing else to do, came back to Lindsay's side.

"We're not busy. Why don't you go ahead and go."

"I think you're trying to get rid of me."

"Don't be ridiculous." But she didn't meet Lindsay's gaze.

"So what did my brother say when he went upstairs?"

"He wanted to tell me what time he'd pick me up tomorrow night."

"Is that all?" Lindsay asked, a teasing look on her face.

"Yes, I think that covered it."

"Is he coming back tonight?"

"Darn! I forgot to mention that I know it's not your mother's birthday for several months. I'll call later and tell him to stay home."

"You think that will work?"

"Of course it will. I'm sure he's tired of spending so much time on me and Drew."

"Whatever you say."

After Lindsay left, Kelly, when the store was empty of customers, dialed the Double C ranch. Carol answered, and Kelly breathed a sigh of relief. "Hi, Carol. I need to leave a message for Pete if you don't mind."

"Hi, Kelly. It's not necessary. He's standing right here."

"No—uh, hi, Pete."

"Hi, Kelly. Miss me already?"

"No! I wanted to make sure you didn't come back to the store tonight."

"Why not? I have that shopping to do, remember?"

"You mean your mother's birthday? It's not until October. I think you have plenty of time."

Pete didn't say anything.

"Look, I know why you were here Monday night, and I appreciate the sentiment, really I do. But I'm a big girl. I can take care of myself. I've closed by myself many a time."

"I don't like it."

"Fortunately it's my job and it has nothing to do with you, so don't show up tonight. You hear?"

"Are you threatening me?"

"Yeah." Then she hung up the phone. She had no idea what she'd do if she had to carry through with that threat. But she'd think of something. She had to. It was time to keep her distance.

* * *

"Another soda, Pete?" the waitress asked.

Pete nodded. He'd already had three colas. The caffeine was going to make him jittery pretty soon. But he was occupying the table, so he had to order something. "Uh, wait, Lucy. Do you have any decaf coffee?"

"Decaf coffee, Pete? I figured you'd drink a few beers. But cola and decaf coffee? What's going on?"

"We all have to grow up sometime. Do you have decaf?" he asked again.

"Sure. I'll bring you a pot. How about some chocolate pie? It's real good tonight."

"Okay, yeah, that'd be good." He looked at his watch. It was only eight-thirty. He had another half hour before Kelly locked her doors. And here, at the pizza place across the street, he had the best view of her store.

He'd decided he'd be smart not to agitate Kelly tonight. So he was keeping his distance, but staying close enough to act if he needed to.

"Hello, lover."

Pete reluctantly took his gaze off the dress store and stared at Sheila Hooten.

"Sheila."

"A little bird told me you were here by yourself. I thought you could use some company."

"No, thanks." He'd gotten way beyond being polite to Sheila.

"So you won't let me sit here with you?" she demanded, surprised.

"Nope. If you do, you'll be telling everyone tomorrow we reconciled. I know how you work and I'm not interested."

She sat down anyway.

He immediately stood and moved one table over. "If you follow me, I'm asking the manager to stop you."

"You wouldn't do that." She moved to his table.

He stood. "Lucy?" he called loudly. "Ask Mac to come out here."

Lucy looked alarmed and Pete knew why. He waited for her to hurry to the table.

"Pete, what's wrong? Mac's busy!"

"This lady won't leave me alone. Because *someone* let her know I was here."

"Oh, Pete, please don't tell Mac. He'll fire me. I didn't mean to do any harm."

"Well, you did. Get her out of here, or I will tell him."

He kept his eyes on the two women, waiting to see who caved in first. Finally, anger on her face, Sheila stomped out of the pizza restaurant.

Lucy came back to his table. "I'm sorry, Pete. She told me you two—"

"Well, she was wrong. Thanks for getting rid of her."

"And you won't tell Mac?"

"No, honey, I won't tell Mac. But don't do it again."

"No. I'll go get your decaf and pie now."

Pete relaxed in his chair and looked across the street at the store. It appeared empty. Then suddenly, two men went in.

Men? Shopping late at a dress shop for women? He

leaped to his feet, dug out a twenty and threw it on the table. Then he ran for the door.

Kelly was sitting behind the counter doing some paperwork when the bell jangled, signifying another customer. She'd sent her mother upstairs since they hadn't done a lot of business tonight after the teenagers went off work.

She regretted that action when she saw two men come in. They almost never had men customers. And this late at night? She wished she hadn't been so stern with Pete.

"Good evening, gentlemen. May I help you?"

Neither of them spoke, making her even more nervous.

Finally the older one muttered, "I need to buy a present."

"For a lady, I hope," Kelly said, relaxing a little.

"Yeah. I forgot our anniversary and went out with Bill here, and if I go home without a present, I'm dead meat."

Kelly relaxed even more. "You're right. Maybe we can think up an excuse as well as a present," she said, stepping over and patting the man's arm. "Tell me about your wife and we'll see what we can do."

"Thanks—" the man began.

The bell over the door jangled wildly and a blur came through the door. It was Pete and he spun the man around and slammed his fist into the customer's nose before Kelly could think of anything to say.

"Pete!" she screamed as the man crumpled to the floor.

"It's okay, Kelly. We'll call the police. You, there, stand back," he ordered to the other man.

The man raised his hands like Pete had a gun. "Why—why'd you do that?" the man asked, his face pale.

"It was obvious," Pete growled.

"Pete, there was no reason. The man was shopping." She reached for the phone and asked her mother to bring down a towel and some ice.

"Shopping? Come on, Kelly. What man shops in a lady's dress shop just before it closes? They're here to rob you."

The man who had taken the blow scooted across the floor away from Pete before he got to his feet. "No, man, that's wrong."

"It's the only reason you'd be here," Pete assured him.

Kelly put her hands on her hips and glared at Pete. "No, it's not. How about a man who forgot his anniversary? He came to get an anniversary present before we closed so his wife wouldn't be mad at him."

Mary came running down the stairs with a bowl of ice and a cup towel. "What's going on?"

No one answered her. Pete stared at the man in horror, and then back at Kelly. "I thought—I mean, I'm sorry, sir. I really thought you were going to rob her. And you'd grabbed her."

"No! I grabbed him. Mom, come help me stop his

nose from bleeding. I'm sorry, sir, but please don't bleed on the clothes, or Pete will have to buy out the store."

Mary recognized the man with the bloody nose. "Hi, Sam. What happened?"

He pointed to Pete. "He thought I was robbing the store."

Kelly apologized again. "I couldn't stop him. I didn't realize what he was thinking until it was too late."

"I didn't want you to get hurt."

Kelly looked at Pete again, but she didn't glare this time. "I know but—"

"Look," Pete said, turning to face the man. "I made a mistake. Let me give you some compensation." He pulled out his wallet.

The man refused. "I really need a present, that's all. Will you help me, please?"

"For Geraldine?" Mary asked.

"Yeah. I forgot our anniversary."

"I know exactly what she wants. She was in this afternoon. She'd hoped to bring you back in tonight."

"Gosh, Mary, that's great. I'll take it." Both men edged their way toward Mary, keeping one eye on Pete.

Mary looked at Pete. "Sam's wife is the one who asked you about buying that knit dress. You suggested blue to match her eyes."

"Oh, nice lady," Pete said, still embarrassed by his mistake. "Look, I'll buy the dress for your wife as an apology."

"No. I have to get her something."

Kelly stepped forward. "Let him pay, Sam. It will

make him feel better. And you use your money to take Geraldine to a nice restaurant tomorrow night where she can wear her new dress. And you can tell her you couldn't get a reservation until tomorrow night. And maybe she'll forgive you."

"I don't deserve for her to forgive me. I feel like a worm."

Mary carried the dress to the cash register and waved Pete over. "How you paying, cowboy? Cash or credit?"

Pete pulled out his credit card and gave it to Mary.

"I'm sure she will forgive you, Sam," Kelly said.

Mary passed the shopping bag with the dress inside over to Sam and his friend. "Good luck, guys. And we'll protect you from Pete the next time you come in."

The two men laughed.

"No hard feelings?" Pete asked, sticking out his hand.

"Naw. I've had a bloody nose before. Don't worry about it."

After they left the store, Mary locked the door. "I think we can close five minutes early after all the excitement."

"Kelly, I really am sorry, but I thought—"

"Where did you come from?" she asked, frowning.

"Uh, I was having pizza across the street."

"Pete, I told you I could take care of myself," Kelly protested.

"Now, dear, I think it's sweet that he thought he was rescuing you from robbers," Mary said.

"Mom, don't encourage him."

"I just wanted to be sure," he said, pleading in his voice, tenderness in his brown eyes.

"I know." Kelly sighed. "Fine, I forgive you. But don't do it again!"

"I'll check things out next time before I throw any punches," he assured her.

"That's not what I meant!"

He grinned, leaned over for a brief kiss and headed for the door, the big grin still pasted on his face.

Chapter Ten

Pete figured he'd made some progress with Kelly. She'd gotten over his mistake quickly. And there was no other man. Definite progress.

He thought about her all day, still rounding up cows. His herd was growing fast. He was thinking about building a house on his land. He should have moved out years ago, but it had been so convenient.

He could put a fence around the backyard so Drew— or any child, he hurriedly thought, could play. He could buy a couple of mares from Rick. His brother was an expert on horses. And maybe a pony.

A cow jumped out of the bushes and ran past him. His horse, a trained cutting horse, took after the cow, almost leaving Pete behind. When he finally rounded up the cow and brought her to the herd, Joe gave him a good stare. "Where's your head, Pete? Your horse almost dumped you."

"Yeah," Pete agreed, clearing his throat. "I guess I was woolgathering."

"Maybe about slugging an innocent man?" Rick asked.

"Dammit, Rick, is listening to gossip all you do?" Pete roared.

"That and work, keeping my mind on my job," Rick said with a big grin.

"What are you talking about this time?" Joe asked.

"Last night, Pete ran into the dress shop and slugged a man because he thought he was trying to rob the store."

"Good for you," Joe said.

"Not really," Rick continued. "The man was shopping for an anniversary present."

"Then why did you hit him?" Joe asked, looking confused.

"I *thought* he was robbing the store."

"Because he had a gun?"

"No. He didn't have a gun."

"Because Kelly held her hands up?"

"No." Pete was feeling harassed. He wanted to tell his brothers to forget it, but he knew from experience they wouldn't.

"Then why?"

"It was late. I couldn't figure out why two men would go to a dress shop right before closing time except to rob it."

Joe shook his head. "I think you'd better marry Kelly before you hurt yourself. You've got to keep your mind on your job...and reality."

"Marry her?" Pete shook his head. "You know I don't intend to marry. And don't you say anything, Joe. You're a year older than me and you still live at home."

Joe nodded. "Yeah, pitiful, isn't it?"

Pete shrugged his shoulders and guided his horse away from the herd. There were more cows to be found before he could pick up Kelly and Drew for the fair.

Kelly knew she'd gone easy on Pete the night before. She also knew she was in trouble. Other than her mother, no one had cared enough about her to try to protect her. It was a seductive feeling. Pete, of course, was just playing the role, but if she wasn't careful, she'd let down her guard. Just when she began to rely on Pete, he'd disappear.

She wore jeans and a knit shirt for the fair. She didn't want Pete to think she was dressing up to go with him. And the linen pants Lindsay suggested she wear would give him that opinion so she wore a pair of jeans.

She'd found a pair of jeans for Drew, too. He looked so cute, like a little boy instead of her baby. He was growing up fast.

"Pete?" he said, looking at his mother.

"Oh, dear. Yes, sweetie, we're going with Pete." She tried to think of something to distract him. "Do you want to go show Grandma your jeans? She'll really like them."

Mary was closing the shop for Kelly because Rafe wouldn't get there until seven, and Pete was coming at six. She grabbed Drew's stuffed monkey he liked to play with and carried him and her son downstairs.

There were still several customers in the store, so Kelly sat Drew on the bottom stair and gave him his monkey. Then she went to the cash register as a customer got ready to pay her bill.

"Your little boy looks darling, Kelly," the older woman said.

"Thank you. We're going to the fair this evening."

"By yourself? I don't think—"

"No. Not by ourselves," she said and put the woman's purchase into a sack. She handed it to her and told her to come again.

"Oh, I will. I guess that means Pete Crawford is going with you. Everyone had just about given up on him marrying. Then Sheila claimed him, and then you. He's a slippery one, so be careful."

"Yes, I will," Kelly said, hoping the lady left before Pete appeared. The sound of the bell over the door told her it was too late. Pete came in and immediately came behind the counter and draped his arm around Kelly.

"Hello, Mrs. Dolittle. How are you?"

"Just fine, Pete," the customer replied, staring at the two of them. "Looks like you're fine, too."

"Sure am." Drew made a noise and Pete turned to find him tugging on his jeans. "Hey, guy. How are you?" He scooped Drew up into his arms. "Ready to go?"

"Well, I must say, I didn't believe the rumors, but I guess they were right. You *are* ready to settle down."

Kelly stood rigidly, saying nothing. Pete laughed and said, "Maybe."

After the woman left, he leaned over and kissed Kelly briefly. "Don't let the gossips upset you. Are you ready?"

Easy for him to say. "I'd like to wait until Mom can close the store. I don't like to leave her alone."

"Sure. Is Drew ready to go? Do I need to do anything?"

She stared at him. Why not? "It would be good if you took him to the bathroom again before we leave."

"He's not wearing diapers?"

"No."

"Way to go, cowboy. Let's go upstairs."

Kelly stood there watching Drew's beaming face over Pete's shoulder. She'd thought Pete would be uncomfortable. Instead he seemed perfectly happy with Drew.

Just what she didn't need.

When they reached the fairground, Pete parked his truck and got Drew out of his car seat. "I'll get the stroller out," Kelly said, opening her door.

"I don't think that's a good idea," Pete said, surprising her.

"Why not?"

"I don't like the idea of him being down low in this crowd. There'll be a lot of dust kicked up into the air. I'll just carry him."

"He's heavy, Pete," she protested.

"Not as heavy as a bale of hay. I'll manage."

Before she could argue, he grabbed her hand and pulled her after him and Drew. For a while, Drew rode on his shoulders, his stubby little legs around Pete's neck.

"I like his blue jeans," Pete said, grinning at Kelly. "Makes him look like a cowboy."

Kelly's smile was wiped away. She said nothing.

"Come on, Kelly, you can't blame all cowboys for your husband's behavior."

She stopped to admire a quilt in one of the booths.

"You like that?" Pete asked, scrutinizing the home-made item.

"It's beautiful work," Kelly said, smiling at the elderly woman sitting behind the counter.

"Thank you," the woman said. "It represents a lot of hours."

"I can imagine." Kelly reached out to stroke the patterned material.

"Are you selling it?" Pete asked.

"Yes, sir. My quilting circle makes them all year and when the fair comes to town, we sell them and give the money to the women's shelter."

"You mean you have more than one?" he asked, peering over the counter.

"We have twelve. I've already sold two."

"Let's see the others," Pete suggested.

"Pete, that's a lot of trouble," Kelly protested. She was doing better financially than she ever had before, but she didn't allow herself frills. A quilt would be a wonderful keepsake, but she could survive without it.

Pete ignored her. "I'm building me a house soon and I think I'd like a quilt for my bed."

Kelly stared at him in surprise. She hadn't heard anything about him building a house.

"Well, we only have two that are king-size. That's the size bed you want, isn't it?"

Pete looked at Kelly, then turned back to the lady and nodded. "You bet. Show me those two."

The woman pulled out two large quilts wrapped in plastic. "One is The Wedding Ring pattern and the other—"

Pete interrupted her. "I'll take that one."

Kelly stared at him as if he'd lost his mind.

"Got plans, do you?" the woman asked with a grin, her gaze flashing from Pete to Kelly and back again.

"Yeah," he grinned. Then some friends stopped by and discovered what he was purchasing. Suddenly they were all abuzz and Kelly understood. This purchase was part of his plan to show them he wasn't marrying Sheila.

For a moment there, her heart had fluttered with the possibility that Pete actually—no, she knew better.

He paid for the quilt and asked the woman to hold it for him until the end of the evening. When they walked away from the quilt booth, he said, "You did like it, didn't you?"

"It's a beautiful quilt. Maybe, when this pretense is over, you can give it to your mother for her birthday."

He ignored her suggestion. "Hey, let's see if I can

win something for Drew," he suggested, stopping in front of the booth where pins were stacked. For a dollar, each participant got three balls. The booth was covered with prizes hanging from the tent walls. Mostly inexpensive stuffed animals.

Pete consulted with Drew and came to the conclusion that Drew would like a prize. He asked Kelly to hold the little boy and plunked down a dollar. It took him no time at all to knock down the first sets of pins. But to win any prize in the booth, he had to knock down five more sets.

Kelly protested, saying a small toy would satisfy her son. Pete ignored her.

When he'd knocked down everything, his face beaming with pride, he took Drew back into his arms and told him to pick out the toy he wanted. There was a teddy bear bigger than any other prize, and Kelly expected her son to reach for it.

Instead Drew reached for a child's red cowboy hat, probably the cheapest prize in the booth. "Hat," Drew said. Then he reached up and touched Pete's Stetson.

"You want that scrawny little hat? But you can have that big bear, if you want it," Pete pointed out.

Drew stubbornly insisted on the hat. When the owner of the booth gave it to Drew, with much relief, Drew put it on his head. Then he turned to smile at Pete. "Me, Pete," he said, touching first Pete's hat and then his new one.

"Aw, Drew, you bet. We're just a couple of cowboys

out on the town, aren't we, buddy?" He turned to face Kelly and said, "What do you think, Mom?"

"Fine," she said faintly and turned away.

He hurriedly thanked the man and caught up with Kelly. "Come on, Kelly, don't be that way. He looks pretty cute in his hat, doesn't he? He'll have to fight off the women when he's older."

"Like you...or his daddy?"

"I don't think I deserve being compared to your ex-husband." All the good-naturedness disappeared. "Drew, give me back the hat. We'll go exchange it for the bear."

Drew, not understanding much except Pete wanted his hat, shook his head no, holding the hat on his head.

"No! Don't. You're right. I was wrong to— His red hat looks fine," Kelly said.

"Actually," Pete said, grinning again, "it's a pretty lousy hat, but I'll get him a good one. Not a red one. No self-respecting cow—I mean, man, would wear a red cowboy hat."

"No, it won't be necessary to buy him another hat. Let's see if he wants to go in the petting zoo." She hurried down the midway and found the entrance. "Drew, do you want to pet the animals?"

Drew leaned out for him mother to take him, his eyes already on the small animals moving around.

Pete held him back. "You'd better let me go in with him. Otherwise, your shoes are going to get messed up."

Kelly looked at the floor of the pen and her white sneakers. There was plenty of evidence to tell her Pete was right. He was wearing boots, of course. "Okay, if you don't mind."

"Naw, I don't mind. Go sit on that bench and watch him."

They spent almost half an hour at the petting zoo. Pete followed Drew around as he petted a goat, a lamb, a foal. He didn't have much interest in the chickens or the ducks. But his favorite animals were the puppies. He plopped down beside the pen at once when Pete offered him a puppy to hold and didn't move. Gently he petted the puppy and hugged it to him. Finally Pete put it back in the pen with its brothers and Drew cried.

It was the first time he'd seen the child upset. His heart almost broke when big, fat tears trailed down Drew's little face. He opened his mouth to promise the boy his very own puppy. Then he remembered they were living in an apartment. And he hadn't consulted Kelly.

He lifted Drew into his arms and consoled him as he hurried outside the fence to reach Kelly. He knew how much she loved Drew and expected her to be upset because her son was disappointed.

Kelly took Drew onto her lap and began cheerfully discussing the baby ducks with her son. Drew finally perked up, and Pete gave a sigh of relief.

They moved on to the kiddie rides. Drew liked the little cars that went round in a circle. He wasn't sure about going off by himself, without Pete or Kelly, but when he discovered they were still there when he came back around, he relaxed and even honked his horn.

Though Pete tried to interest him in other rides, Drew kept asking for the cars.

After the third time on the cars, Kelly said she was ready for a corn dog.

"But Drew wants to ride again," Pete pointed out, a frown on his face.

"I know. But three times is enough. Drew, do you want to eat?"

Distracted, Drew nodded and soon they were sitting at a picnic table with corn dogs, drinks and hot French fries.

"Not the healthiest meal in the world," Pete said, a little worried.

"Relax, Pete. We don't do this every night." She was keeping an eye on her son.

"You're really good at this mother thing," he finally said.

She looked up. "What?"

"You're good at doing what's best. He almost broke my heart over those puppies."

"Children have to learn that they can't have everything they want."

"I agree, but all little boys should have a puppy."

"Did you have one?"

"I had three or four. We've always had dogs on the ranch. My first one I named Marshmallow. He was white. Dad made me take care of him. It was a good learning experience. Drew could—"

"Not have a dog," she finished. "We're in an apartment, Pete. It isn't possible."

"What if you moved into a house?" Pete asked, his jaw squaring.

"I don't think that's going to happen. Things are going well right now, but that's because I get the apartment so cheaply from Lindsay. I can't afford a house."

Pete looked as if he was going to continue to argue, but she was grateful when he didn't. But he pressed his lips tightly together.

"More!" Drew ordered as he reached the end of his corn dog.

"I don't think so. Have a French fry," Kelly suggested. She offered one to Drew and he took it and shoved it into his mouth. "Your manners are atrocious, you little monster," she teased.

Drew beamed at her.

"I'll feed him while you finish your corn dog," Pete suggested.

"Thanks. But make him chew each one up before you give him another one." She'd learned that lesson the hard way.

After they finished eating, Kelly pulled out the sanitary wipes to clean her son. In seconds, he was as clean as he'd been at the beginning of the evening.

That, of course, was before Pete introduced Drew to cotton candy. After about two seconds, Drew dived headfirst into the pink, sticky mass. Kelly did another wipe job, trying to get the sticky sugar out of Drew's eyelashes and hair. She scrubbed his hands, too.

"I think you'd better hand-feed him a little piece at a time," she said, showing Pete what she meant.

"You've got the patience of a saint. I'm sorry, Kelly, it didn't occur to me that he'd do such a thing."

"The good thing about little boys is that they're completely washable. I only hope he doesn't get it all over your clothes."

"I'm washable, too," he assured her.

Kelly couldn't help but return his smile. She was having a wonderful time.

"If you want to go on some of the big rides, or—visit with some of your friends, Drew and I can wait here," she suddenly offered, realizing he might not be as crazy about spending his Friday evening with her and her child. "Or you could take us home and come back."

"I'm ready to go if you are," he said at once, surprising her.

So, he was missing his bachelor ways. She shouldn't be surprised. She'd warned herself. "Of course. It's past Drew's bedtime. Thank you, though, Pete. We've had a wonderful time."

"Me, too. It's fun watching Drew experience things for the first time."

He wrapped an arm around Kelly's shoulder, carrying Drew in his other arm. They moved slowly back toward where they'd parked his truck, stopping only to pick up the quilt he'd bought.

Kelly took Drew in her arms, and his head fell on her shoulder. It took both Pete's arms to carry the big quilt. It was gorgeous. Pete could decorate his bedroom around the quilt. Some sky-blue curtains to pick up the blue in the quilt. What a heavenly idea.

"Here we are," Pete pointed out. He put the quilt in the back of the truck and unlocked the door. Taking Drew from her, he slid him into the car seat that separated the two adults. "Hey, buddy, are you asleep? We're heading for home, so just hang on."

He helped Kelly in and rounded the truck quickly to start the drive home.

"You're not going to leave the quilt back there, are you? Someone might steal it when you come back to the fair."

He turned to stare at her. "Come back to the fair? What are you talking about?"

"I thought you were taking us home and then going back to be with your friends." She didn't look at him because she didn't want him to see how much she wanted him to deny that plan.

"Drew and I are going to play in his bathwater," Pete corrected. "Then we'll tuck him in, read him a story. Then I'll be ready for a good movie on television and maybe some homemade popcorn. Do you have any?"

"Yes. Are you sure?"

"Yeah, I'm sure."

"Okay," she said sedately. Inside, happiness spread through her. She suddenly wondered if Pete would take off his shirt to bathe Drew.

That intriguing thought kept her tongue-tied all the way home.

Chapter Eleven

Kelly sat at her breakfast table early the next morning, a frown on her face, when Mary entered the room.

She was smiling dreamily.

"Did you have a good time, Mom?"

"Oh, yes, lovely. And you?"

"Too good."

"What do you mean?" Mary asked, studying her daughter closely.

"Pete was wonderful. He pretended to perfection. He took care of Drew like he was his own son. And when we came back and put Drew to bed, we popped corn and watched a movie on television."

"But that sounds nice."

"Of course it was nice! That's what was wrong. He's too good at this!" Tears filled Kelly's eyes and she looked away.

"Oh, honey," Mary said, reaching out to catch her daughter's hand. "You've fallen in love with him."

"I've fallen in love with a figment of my imagination. I promised myself I wouldn't ever be so foolish again." She covered her face with her hands.

"It's not the same, Kelly." Mary waited silently, but Kelly couldn't speak.

"Pete's a good man. He keeps his word."

"He hasn't promised me anything, Mom. We're pretending and we both know it. I didn't think—" she gulped before she could continue "—I thought I could handle being around him. I thought I was man-proof."

"No one is able to resist all men or women. I figured that out long ago. I worry about falling for Rafe so quickly. Is it because I've been so lonely? But you know, I'm not sure I care anymore. I just want to be with him. So at least for a while, I'll truly be happy. And if I'm lucky, it might last forever."

Kelly reached out and took her mother's hand. "I hope so, Mom. You deserve to be happy for the rest of your life more than anyone I know."

"But you do, too, Kelly. You're such a good mother, a good daughter, a hard worker."

"If I'm a good mother, I should take Drew and run for the hills. I shouldn't expose my son to a broken heart."

"Are you sure it's Drew you're worrying about?" Mary finally asked.

Kelly stared at her mother, upset with her words. Before she could protest, however, someone knocked on their door. She checked her watch, but it was too early for Lindsay to arrive.

She wiped her eyes and found a tissue to blow her nose. Then she opened the door to discover Pete leaning against the door frame.

"Hey, Kel, did I wake you up?"

"No! No, I'm awake." She quickly turned her back to him. "Do you want a cup of coffee?"

"Hey, that'd be great. Black, please."

"Mom, would you heat up some of those muffins you baked yesterday? We can all have breakfast." She figured the more she distracted him, the easier it would be to keep him from noticing her red eyes until she recovered.

"Is Drew still asleep?" he asked.

"Yes. I'm sure he was tired from the fair." She kept her back to him.

"I have a proposition to make," he said after a minute.

Even Kelly turned around. Mary asked the question. "What?"

"I thought the store might be really busy today. So Mom suggested I pick up Drew and let him spend the day with me at the ranch. Which means Mary can help out whenever she's needed."

"That would be great," Mary said, "but keeping track of a toddler is tough. You can't do much else."

"It's not a good idea," Kelly said, turning her back again.

"Why?" he asked.

A simple question. But one she didn't want to answer. She brought his coffee to the table. As she turned back toward the sink, he caught her wrist.

"What's wrong, Kelly?" he asked quietly.

"Nothing! I don't know what you're talking about." She pulled on his hold and he let her go. She retreated to the sink, her back to him once again.

Mary brought the muffins to the table. "These are banana nut, Pete. I hope you like them."

"I'm sure I will."

"Mama?" Drew's voice drew everyone's attention, all three adults turning to the door to Drew's room. The little boy pushed his way through, rubbing his eyes as he walked into the kitchen. Then he saw their guest.

"Pete!" Drew exclaimed. He ran to Pete to point out the obvious. "Hat!" He was wearing his red cowboy hat.

"My, where did you get that fine hat?" Mary asked with a smile.

Drew patted Pete's knee. "Pete."

Pete picked him up and sat him in his lap. "Okay for Drew to share my muffin?" he asked.

"Yes, of course. I'll get him some milk," Kelly said.

She could feel Pete's gaze on her back, but she was determined to keep him at a distance. She brought the milk to the table for Drew.

"Thank you for your offer, but Drew isn't used to being separated from either Mom or me. And she's right. It's impossible to do much when he's with you. You haven't worked much this week because of us. We don't want to cause you any more difficulty."

"Work isn't a problem," Pete assured her.

She shook her head.

"Mom will be there to help me."

"I'm sure your mother has forgotten how difficult it is to take care of young children."

"Kelly, that's the most ridiculous thing you've ever said," Pete protested. "Tell me you don't trust me. But don't lie to me."

"I don't trust you," she repeated, her voice leaden.

A tense silence filled the room.

Mary suddenly took Drew from Pete. "Come on, pumpkin. Let's go get you dressed." Without saying anything else, she left Kelly alone with Pete.

He rose and came up behind her as she stood at the sink. Taking her shoulders in his hands, he turned her around to face him.

"You've been crying. Why?"

She didn't like being forced to lie, but she had no choice unless she wanted to confess that she'd forgotten they were pretending, she would.

"It's that time of the month!" she snapped.

"You know if you have a problem, I'll help you, don't you?" he asked, ignoring her tacky lie.

"It's not required. I'll keep my promise anyway," she assured him. "However, I think you should be safe very soon." She kept her gaze lowered, even though he stood close to her.

His hand came under her chin to force her face up. "Won't you tell me what's wrong?"

"I told you nothing is wrong. I just have a long day before me."

"Let Drew come with me. He'll have a good time and it will give you and your mom a break."

"No!"

"Why?"

"I told you—"

"I don't believe you."

She looked at him, or glared at him more like. "I don't want him to get too fond of you, Pete! When our pretense is over, he'll want to know where you are. He can't spend any more time with you. It will hurt him!"

As she finished, the door opened and Drew flew into the kitchen, squealing Pete's name.

Pete frowned before he displayed a smile for Drew. Taking him in his big hands, he lifted him into the air and caught him. Drew loved it.

"I'm sorry, Kelly. I know what you're saying. I've told you I'll still want to see him. And he's already...he likes to be with me." He sighed and faced her. "One more day won't hurt and you can get a break. Please let me take him."

"I don't think it will hurt," Mary added.

Kelly turned her back to Pete again, silently cursing her weakness even as she agreed. "If he wants to."

"Hey, pal, want to go see my horse and lots of cows while Mama works? Then we'll take her to dinner this evening."

"Are you sure we haven't convinced Sheila already?" Kelly asked, weakly, half of her wanting him to agree, and the other half, knowing she wouldn't see him anymore, hoping he wouldn't.

"Not yet."

"Fine. I have to go down and clean up."

Mary protested and Pete called for her to wait, but she ignored them and went downstairs.

"Mary, what's wrong?" Pete asked, still holding Drew.

Mary ducked her head. Then she looked at Pete. "I can't tell you, Pete."

"Can't or won't?"

With a sigh, Mary admitted, "Won't. I can't betray Kelly."

"Is there anything I can do to help? I'll do whatever I can to make everything all right."

"Life's not that simple. Just take good care of our little boy."

"You know I will. Are you ready to go, Drew? Tell Grandma goodbye and we'll go find more animals to talk to. Okay?"

Drew nodded vigorously. Pete grabbed his car seat to take with them.

Mary said, "Wait. I'll get you some spare clothes in case, uh, there's need."

"Good idea." He stood there, holding the little boy, wishing he knew what was really wrong. Wishing he had the right to hold Kelly in his arms until she broke down and told him the truth.

It couldn't be his behavior last night. He'd been very careful to keep it casual. He hadn't kissed her until he was ready to leave, knowing if he did so earlier, he might lose control.

His mother had told him Kelly, Mary and Drew were coming to Sunday dinner. She suggested he call and offer to pick them up after church. He hadn't wanted to stay away today. But he hadn't even brought that subject up. Not when he could tell Kelly had been crying.

Mary emerged with the extra clothes in a small bag. Pete took them, allowed Drew to kiss his grandmother goodbye, and hurried down the stairs to his truck.

Once Drew was strapped into his seat, Pete drove away, still fighting the urge to try one more time to find out what was wrong with Kelly.

All day, Pete played with Drew, taking him to pet the horses, showing him the cows, explaining all kinds of things about being a cowboy, little or any that Drew understood. But the boy was happy.

When Pete took him to the barn and showed him the batch of puppies born a couple of weeks ago, Drew didn't want to look at anything else. He picked out the smallest puppy and sat down in the straw and held it, as he had the night before. The puppy seemed to like the attention. He cuddled up in Drew's lap and licked his hands.

Drew giggled and Pete chuckled. He knew then he

had to become Drew's daddy. He loved Kelly. She wasn't like other women. She was honest, hardworking, beautiful without artifice and loving. He felt about her differently than he ever had about a woman. His vow to remain single didn't stand a chance when it came to Kelly.

What amazed him most of all was it wasn't about sex. Oh, he was sure sex would be great. But he wanted to be there for Kelly. To help her solve her problems. To take care of her and Drew. To be together for the rest of their lives.

He regretted the years he'd wasted. He and Kelly lived in the same area. Why hadn't he realized how he might feel about her a long time ago? But then, maybe she wasn't the same person. She hadn't been hurt. He wished he could make those difficult times go away, but he wouldn't change Kelly for anything.

"Drew, we've got to go eat lunch with Grammy," he said without thinking, using the term Logan's children used for his mother. If he married Kelly and Drew became his little boy, he'd call Carol Grammy, too.

Drew ignored his suggestion, only cuddling more closely with the puppy.

Pete grinned. He knew Kelly would handle things differently, but Pete couldn't bring himself to take the puppy away from the boy. "Okay, tell you what, we'll take the puppy with us and see if Grammy will let you hold it in the house."

He swung the boy and the dog into his arms and marched across the yard.

"Grammy?" he called as he entered.

Carol stepped out of the kitchen to stare at her son. "What did you call me?"

"Grammy. Isn't that what your grandchildren call you?"

"Yes, Logan's children do." She waited for his response.

"I thought maybe we should start Drew off right. And he has a question for you."

Carol broke into a broad smile. "You and Kelly have worked things out?"

"No, but we will. Drew?"

As if he understood what was needed, Drew tried to give the puppy to the lady. "Puppy!"

"I see. Do you like the puppy?"

Pete leaned closer to his mother. "I thought maybe he could hold the dog while we eat lunch."

"I'm not sure his mother will approve," Carol said, taking the puppy before Drew dropped it and cuddling the dog on her shoulder. Drew immediately reached for her, wanting to be with the dog.

She took him in one arm, holding the dog with the other. Drew reached for the dog and settled against her, a beaming smile on his face.

"My, he is adorable. I see why you didn't want to make him give up the puppy. But you're going to pay the price when it's time to go this afternoon."

"I know." Pete sighed. "But I can't help myself. Last night I had to take the puppy away from him at the fair.

He sat there sobbing these big old tears. I thought my heart was going to break.''

"You've got a lot to learn about being a daddy.''

"Yeah, but Kelly can teach me. She's really good with Drew.''

"Okay. Take Drew to the bathroom and clean up. We'll let Mr. Puppy join us for lunch.''

"Oh, my gosh, I forgot.'' Pete grabbed Drew and raced for the bathroom.

Carol chuckled. She remembered those potty-training days and wished him luck.

Kelly was exhausted by the end of the day. All she'd done was worry about Drew. And Pete. They'd been busy in the store, of course, and Lindsay had gone home at two o'clock. The teenagers had gone home at four. She and Mary had carried on until six. Several customers lingered a little longer, but finally she was able to lock the door at 6:20.

She'd expected Pete to have returned by six. Now, she stared out the door, looking for his pickup.

"Mom, Pete's not here yet. Do you think something's wrong?''

Mary, straightening the racks, looked over her shoulder. "No, dear, I don't, but you can call Carol and ask.''

Without a word, Kelly flew to the phone and dialed the number she'd called all her teenager years to discuss everything with Lindsay.

"Carol, this is Kelly. Is Pete there?''

"No, dear. I told him he should call you, but Drew was unhappy and he was already late and—"

"Drew was unhappy?" Kelly interrupted anxiously. "Why was he unhappy?"

"Pete took the puppy away."

Kelly groaned. "I didn't know you had any puppies."

"Oh, we almost always have puppies. Caleb keeps four or five dogs to work with the cattle. Drew took a particular fancy to the smallest puppy. They seemed to bond. Pete's not used to telling Drew 'no.' But he'll get better."

Kelly ignored the inference that Drew would continue to spend time with Pete. "I appreciate you inviting Drew for the day. I know it was a huge imposition and—"

"Not at all. He's adorable. But actually, Pete's the one who spent the day with him. They had a great time. Pete even bathed him and put his extra set of clothes on him so he'd be clean for dinner."

"Oh, I don't think—I'm sure Pete's too tired for dinner after chasing after Drew all day."

"Are you kidding? He'll be starving. As will Drew. You know how growing boys are," Carol added with a laugh.

"Yes, I do. Thanks again." She hurriedly hung up the phone.

"Everything all right?" Mary asked.

"Yes. Drew got unhappy when Pete took a puppy away from him. That made them run late." Kelly moved back to the front door, her gaze still anxious.

With a change of subject, Mary said, "Rafe is coming

to the Double C tomorrow for lunch, too. It's very nice of Carol to invite him.''

''I think he gets invited to all the Crawford functions, sort of as if he were Gil's father.''

''Yes,'' Mary said, her expression dreamy as it had been that morning. ''If I married Rafe, I'd have two grandbabies—Drew, and Lindsay and Gil's child.''

Kelly stared at her mother. It was the first time her mother had mentioned that word. ''Are you and Rafe— have you discussed marriage?''

Mary flushed. ''I—we have. But we're trying to be practical and give everything a little more time. It would involve a lot of change.''

Kelly drew a deep breath. ''Yes, it would, but don't let me and Drew get in your way. You've sacrificed more than any mother should have to for me. I want you to be happy.''

Mary flew across the room to hug her daughter. ''Honey, don't worry. We'll all be happy.''

''Sure, Mom.''

The sound of brakes squealing had Kelly turning back toward the door. Drew and Pete had arrived. She dashed out the door. By the time she reached the truck, Pete had Drew out of the truck in his arms.

''Drew!'' she called, reaching for him.

He dived into her arms and buried his face in her hair, wailing, ''Puppy.''

''Sorry, Kelly. I goofed up. I let him play with a puppy all day and he didn't like leaving it behind,'' Pete said.

"It's all right. I know he's spoiled. But at least you didn't bring the puppy here to talk me into adopting it."

"I thought about it," he admitted with a wry grin. "But I knew it wouldn't work. A boy needs a puppy, but a puppy needs a place to play."

"Thank you."

"Are you and your mom all finished? I'll take both of you over to the pizza place. Drew can eat pizza, can't he?"

"Yes, but—"

"Pissa!" Drew yelled. He'd had it a few times, when Kelly and her mother had been too tired to cook.

"Look, it cheered him up. Come on, Kelly, get your mom and let's get over there before the crowd. After all, it's Saturday night."

Kelly unlocked the store door. "Mom, Pete wants us to go eat pizza with him."

"Oh, I guess I forgot to tell you that Rafe is taking me out tonight. You two go ahead. I'll see you tomorrow afternoon, Pete."

"Yeah, I'll pick all of you up after church," Pete agreed, not disturbed by Mary's desertion.

But Kelly was. "I can fix something for Drew upstairs. I know you must be tired so—"

"You're going to send me home without dinner?" he asked, sounding like she would be committing murder if she did something like that.

"I don't have—I need to do the grocery shopping before I can cook dinner for anyone and I'm just too tired tonight," she explained.

"That's why we should go have pizza," Pete insisted.

"Oh, go on, Kelly," Mary insisted. "You know Drew loves it. And we were certainly busy enough to tire everyone out."

"Fine," she said stiffly. "We'll go eat. Then *I'll* take Drew home and put him to bed." She hoped Pete got the message that he wasn't invited.

Chapter Twelve

Whatever had been wrong this morning hadn't gone away. Pete kept an eye on Kelly, wondering if he dared ask again what was upsetting her.

She was busy settling Drew in his high chair, asking him questions about his day.

"Puppy," Drew said, summing up the day as far as he was concerned.

"You played with a puppy? How nice. Did you take a nap?"

He nodded and said again, "Puppy."

She stared at her son, then looked accusingly at Pete. "Is he saying he took a nap with the puppy?"

"Aw, Kelly, he probably doesn't even understand what you asked." Pete avoided looking at her, afraid she'd see something in his gaze.

She gave him a hard stare, but then turned back to her son. "Did you eat a good lunch?"

Pete started to answer, afraid Drew would say puppy again. He hadn't let the boy feed the dog table scraps, but he had let him hold him.

"Grammy! Puppy!" Drew said with a big smile.

"Who's Grammy?" she asked Pete.

"Uh, that's what little children call my mother." He watched Kelly's face cloud up. Time to take charge before things got worse.

"The waitress is coming. What kind of pizza do you want? Does Drew need cheese pizza?"

"Yes. And I'll have that, too."

"Come on, honey, you want something more on your pizza than cheese."

"It will save money if I share with Drew."

"I don't care about that. Do you like sausage, hamburger, pepperoni, anchovies?"

She shuddered. "No anchovies. Other than that, I eat most toppings."

Lucy, the same waitress from Thursday night, arrived at their table, ready to take the order. She said hello to Pete and smiled at Kelly. "Cute little boy. Is he having pizza, too?"

"Yeah. We want a small cheese pizza for him and a large pepperoni, hamburger and Canadian bacon pizza with extra cheese."

"Drinks?"

Pete looked at Kelly.

She said, "Iced tea for me and a small milk for Drew."

"I'll have iced tea, too," Pete added, smiling at Lucy.

"Do you want the chocolate pie you paid for Thursday night?"

Kelly looked surprised. Pete shrugged his shoulders. "We'll see."

After Lucy had walked away, Kelly asked, "What chocolate pie?"

"I'd just ordered some chocolate pie when I saw those two men enter the store. I didn't hang around to eat my dessert."

"You should have," Kelly returned, with the hint of a smile that relieved Pete's concern.

"Yeah. Tell me how your day went. Did you make a lot of sales?"

"Yes, more than I expected. The store is doing very well."

"Maybe soon you should hire a manager."

She stared at him. "Hire a manager? What do you think I am?"

"A busy lady. You know Lindsay won't ever be back full-time after the baby's born. You can't carry the load alone."

"Mother helps me."

"Maybe not for much longer. You know Rafe is crazy about her, don't you?"

She stared out the window across the street at her store. "Yes, and I'm happy for her. But I'll manage."

He decided he shouldn't say anything more on that

subject until he'd discussed other things with Kelly. But he wanted to wait until she was in a good mood.

Lucy brought their drinks. After setting them down, she said, "I'm not calling anyone tonight, Pete. I just wanted you to know."

"Thanks, Lucy. I appreciate that."

Kelly looked at him questioningly.

After Lucy left, he said, "She called Sheila the other night to tell her I was here alone. Sheila showed up."

"What happened?"

"She wanted to sit down at my table. I threatened to call the manager. Lucy was afraid she'd be fired, so she convinced Sheila to go."

"You could've let her sit down, Pete," Kelly chastised him.

"Nope. She would've told everyone we'd reconciled. I wasn't having any of that."

"Surely she wouldn't—"

"Yeah, she would have. Most women aren't as honorable and truthful as you are, sweetheart."

"I don't feel honest. This stupid pretense has gone on much longer than I expected it to."

"It will be over soon."

A long silence fell between them. Pete couldn't imagine his life without her and Drew in it. He wanted to tell her that, but he was afraid she'd run out of the pizza place screaming. Sometimes he wasn't sure she liked him at all. Other times, they were perfect together, like when they watched the movie last night. Or when he kissed her.

Lucy came hurrying across the room, carrying the small pizza for Drew and the large one for the adults. She set them down, warned about them being hot, and went back for plates.

After Lucy set them down, she stood there.

Pete looked up. ''Did you want me to pay now, Lucy?''

''Oh, no! But—but I got a call while I was in the back.''

Pete stiffened. ''Don't tell me Sheila's coming.''

''No. You won't have to worry about her again. She eloped tonight.''

Pete froze, staring at Kelly.

Her eyes got big. He couldn't tell if the news made her happy or sad. ''Uh, thanks for letting me know, Lucy.''

''No problem. Enjoy your pizza.''

After another look at Kelly, he figured that was unlikely.

''It's over,'' Kelly said quietly. Then she turned to deal with her son who was demanding his dinner.

Pete watched her cut up bites of pizza, blowing on them to be sure they were cool enough for her son. She put a saucerful in front of Drew and let him eat with his hands. He stopped protesting at once.

Then she reached for a piece of the big pizza, sliding it onto her plate.

''I guess you can tell your mother why we won't be there tomorrow,'' she said softly, not looking at him.

"No! I can't. She's already fixed enough food to feed an army. She'd be hurt if you didn't come."

"You didn't tell her we were—"

"No!" He hated the word pretending. "I didn't. So she'd be insulted if you didn't show. Besides, what's one more day? You'll get a great meal out of it, and Drew can see the puppy again."

As he'd figured, Drew recognized that word and beamed, repeating it over and over.

"Eat your dinner, Drew," Kelly ordered. "But, Pete—"

"Kelly, give me tomorrow. After that, it's over. You've been great, but I won't ask you to pretend anymore. After tomorrow."

He had something to show her. And to ask her. He hoped and prayed her answer would be yes. How he'd sleep tonight, he didn't know. His entire future would be decided tomorrow.

Kelly felt as if she'd scarcely slept. All night long she'd tossed and turned, thinking about her life without Pete. Wondering how she'd get through tomorrow without breaking into tears.

How humiliating. Becoming only one of many women who had fallen for Pete, only to be dismissed. Would he think he'd have to "pretend" with another woman? No, she'd made sure he understood that she'd be okay. She wouldn't pursue him. She'd told him she didn't want to wed. She wasn't changing her mind. Because the only man she wanted to wed was the least likely one to ever exchange those permanent vows.

In church, she and her mother slipped inside to sit in the back. She'd run late getting ready. After dropping Drew off at the nursery, they discovered the service had already begun.

"The Crawfords are in their usual pew," Mary leaned over to whisper. "Rafe is with them."

Kelly knew where they were. She looked away.

"Pete and Rafe have seen us," Mary whispered again.

Kelly shushed her mother, afraid she'd draw attention to them. And she still didn't look at the Crawfords. So she was surprised when Pete and Rafe, during the so-prano's solo, appeared at the end of their row. Pete came in first, climbing over several couples and her mother to sit down beside her. Rafe followed, only he sat down on the other side of Mary.

"I thought you weren't going to make it," Pete whis-pered in her ear, wrapping his arm around her shoulders.

"Pete, this isn't necessary!" Kelly whispered fiercely. She didn't need such a sweet reminder about what she would be missing after today.

He kissed her on her ear and turned his face inno-cently forward, as if he were paying rapt attention to the soloist.

Kelly didn't know whether to laugh or cry. She should pull away from Pete, but no one seemed to be noticing. If she pulled away, it would draw attention to them. Besides, she didn't want to publicly dump Pete. Not after

Sheila eloped with another man after telling everyone she was going to marry Pete.

Was that what he was going to ask her? That they stay together a little longer so people wouldn't feel sorry for him? No, that couldn't be true. He'd said if she would just pretend today, she wouldn't have to pretend anymore.

When the service ended, Pete grabbed her hand. "I'll go with you to get Drew. Do you have the car seat in your car?"

"Yes. So there's no need for you to drive us out to the ranch. I'll drive us out."

"Mary's going with Rafe. And I'm driving you and Drew. I'll follow you back to your place. We'll transfer the car seat to my truck. Then we'll be on our way."

"You don't mind, do you, dear?" Mary asked, still holding Rafe's hand.

If Kelly insisted on driving herself, it would upset her mother, she supposed. She wanted her mother to be happy. Okay, so she was looking for excuses to be with Pete. But it was just for one more day. "Okay, that's fine. I just hate for Pete to drive back into town later today."

Pete grinned. "I think I can manage a five-mile drive."

She gave an awkward nod, wanting to drop the subject.

When they reached the door to the nursery, Drew saw Pete and ran across the room, his arms held out, calling Pete's name.

"Hey, cowboy, are you ready to go?"

"Weady!" Drew assured him.

Pete picked him up and Kelly took the diaper bag she'd left for emergencies.

Pete leaned over and whispered, "How's he doing?"

"Very well," she returned.

They started down the hall. "I thought potty-training was supposed to be really hard."

Kelly rolled her eyes. "It is."

When they got back to the apartment, Pete transferred the car seat to his truck while Kelly took Drew upstairs. They were back in minutes, Drew dressed in jeans again and wearing his red hat.

Kelly shrugged her shoulders. "He insisted."

Though Pete wasn't wearing a suit, only a nice shirt and slacks, he wore his Stetson. Drew had noticed when Pete picked him up at the nursery.

In Pete's truck, they drove to the ranch. About half a mile from the house, Pete stopped the truck.

"What is it?" Kelly asked at once. "Is something wrong with the truck?"

"No. But this is what I wanted to show you." He waved his hand toward her window.

Kelly stared out at the pasture land. There were several big trees in this particular spot. It was pretty, but not much different from other range land. She turned to stare at Pete. "What?"

"This is my place."

She blinked at him several times. Then she turned to

stare at the land again. "It's—it's very nice. I didn't know you owned any land."

"Yeah. I'm going to build my house right here, on the corner, so I'll have neighbors in sight."

"Your parents? That will be nice. So you really are going to build a house."

"Yeah. Do you like this place?"

"It's lovely."

"How many bedrooms, do you think?"

"How many do I think? Pete, that should be your decision."

"I reckon you should participate." He drew a deep breath, as if he were nervous. "'Cause I'm not building it unless you'll join me, you and Drew."

She'd prepared herself to say goodbye. To put him out of her life. Now she shook her head. "What?"

"Are you saying no?" he asked, his face anxious. "Wait, Kelly don't—"

"I wasn't saying no. I don't know what you asked."

He leaned around Drew's car seat and grabbed one hand. "I'm saying I love you. I'm asking you to marry me."

"No. You're not. You're the least likely person in the world to get married. Remember? You told me you'd never marry."

"You told me that, too. But I'm hoping you'll change your mind. Because no one but you can convince me to walk down that aisle."

"Pete, I can't risk—I want forever, not just a year or

two.'' Or six months of misery as she'd had the first time.

"It had better be forever, sweetheart. I'm only marrying once, because you're the only one for me."

"Are you serious?" she asked, tears filling her eyes.

He unsnapped her seat belt and pulled her over to his lap. Drew squealed, apparently thinking they were playing a game. He held out his arms to Pete, too.

"Not now, cowboy. Your mom needs my attention," Pete muttered to the child just before he kissed her. A deep kiss, one that made her crazy with longing. She wrapped her arms around his neck and pressed against him, which made him kiss her even more.

"Oh, Pete, are you sure?"

"How about you? Are you sure? I want to be with you and Drew and any other children we might have, forever. I want to wake up beside you each morning and kiss you good-night every night. I want to teach Drew everything a cowboy needs to know."

She buried her face in his shirt. "A cowboy?"

"Don't doubt it, sweetheart. A cowboy is faithful, loving, and protects his own. You and Drew are going to be mine, forever."

"You don't mind that Drew isn't really yours?" she asked anxiously. She had to provide for her son, even if it meant giving up Pete.

"He's mine. Your ex-husband may have provided the sperm, but I'm going to be doing the raising."

"Pete!" Drew protested, patting him on the shoulder with his little hand.

"Tired of this sissy stuff, guy? Give you fifteen years. 'Course, we'll have to have a talk about how to treat a lady long before that," Pete said grinning.

"Pete!" Drew repeated.

"You're going to have to learn a new word, son," Pete said, grinning at the little boy. "You need to start calling me Daddy. Okay? Can you say that?"

Drew stared at him.

Pete looked at Kelly. "Okay with you, Mom?"

With her arms around his neck, tears in her eyes, she lay her head on his shoulder. "Okay with me, my love."

"Hey, that's even better than Daddy," Pete assured her as the least likely cowboy to wed kissed the least likely lady to say yes.

Epilogue

Pete had Drew in the bath when Kelly got home. She wasn't working nights at the store, but she and Lindsay had gone to Dallas on a buying trip. A lot of things had changed in the past two years, including their new house, Lindsay and Gil's little girl, and Rafe and Mary's wedding. But, best of all was his life with Kelly and Drew.

"Guys?" Kelly called as she came in the door.

Pete's heart raced. She was home. He didn't like it when she was out of town. "In here," he called down the stairs.

"Mama's home!" Drew exclaimed, jumping up too fast, spreading water all over the room. Then he almost fell as he lost his footing.

"Good thing I caught you, cowboy, or you would've sent a tidal wave all over the place and Mama would be unhappy."

He wrapped him in a towel and went out into the hallway to watch Kelly come up.

"Did everything go all right?" she asked.

"Now that you're home, you bet. Mom and Mary stopped and checked on us all the time. But we were fine, weren't we, Drew?"

"Daddy burned the oatmeal," Drew said, laughing.

"Oh, he did? I thought you told me you could cook," she said, smiling.

"Close enough." He put Drew on the floor and swept Kelly into his arms as she reached the top of the stairs.

"Mama has to kiss me!" Drew protested. "I'm her boy."

"I thought you were my boy," Pete said, still holding Kelly against him, wondering how he'd made it three days without touching her.

"Yeah, but I'm Mama's boy, too."

"Oh, okay. Let's get your pj's on. It's time for you to hit the hay."

"I want to stay up with Mama."

Pete opened his mouth to protest, knowing he wouldn't be satisfied until after Drew was in bed.

Kelly answered before he could. "I'll read you a story as soon as you're dressed. I brought you a new book."

Drew cheered and ran for the bathroom, losing the towel halfway there.

"He's a modest child," Kelly said with a grin.

"Oh, yeah, and fortunately he's fast. It won't take long for him to go to sleep tonight. I wore him out today."

He loved it when she smiled at him like that, as if she were in perfect agreement.

Twenty minutes later, he took her to bed. Drew had fallen asleep faster than ever. After they made love, Pete held Kelly against him. "I missed you."

"I'm glad. I missed you, too."

"Did the trip go all right?"

"Sort of," Kelly said calmly.

Pete rose on one elbow. "What do you mean, sort of?"

"Well, I had to go to the emergency room because I fainted."

His heart almost stopped beating. "What's wrong? We'll go to Oklahoma City tomorrow, see the best doctors. We'll—"

"We'll do no such thing. I'll be fine."

"But why did you faint?" he demanded, not satisfied.

"Because I'm pregnant, honey, that's all."

She said those magic words so offhandedly, so calmly, he couldn't take them in for a moment. Then he repeated faintly, "You're pregnant?"

She beamed at him. "Yes. Okay?"

"Okay? I'm ecstatic! Over the moon! Mom's going to be so excited. Are you sure you're all right?"

"I couldn't be better," Kelly said with a satisfied smile. "For a woman who never intended to marry, I'm doing pretty well for myself."

"Not nearly as well as a man who stupidly thought marrying would be a bad thing," he said, cuddling her against him.

"When our boys get old enough, I'm going to set them straight about marriage so they won't make the same mistake."

"Are you so sure we're having a boy?"

"Do you know? Are we having a girl? A girl that guys will want to— Oh, no! She's not dating until she's thirty, at least!"

"Then how will we get grandchildren?"

"But I don't think—you're right. But only cowboys, okay? She can only date cowboys."

"As long as they're like her daddy, I couldn't agree more."

* * * * *

*There are plenty more
Judy Christenberry titles
in the works. Watch for*
THE RANDALLS: WYOMING WINTER,
*a special two-stories-in-one reissue
on sale in March,
and an original Harlequin American Romance,*
RANDALL RICHES,
on sale in April.

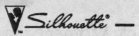

This Mother's Day Give Your Mom A Royal Treat

Win a fabulous one-week vacation in Puerto Rico for you and your mother at the luxurious Inter-Continental San Juan Resort & Casino. The prize includes round trip airfare for two, breakfast daily and a mother and daughter day of beauty at the beachfront hotel's spa.

INTER·CONTINENTAL
San Juan
RESORT & CASINO

Here's all you have to do:

Tell us in 100 words or less how your mother helped with the romance in your life. It may be a story about your engagement, wedding or those boyfriends when you were a teenager or any other romantic advice from your mother. The entry will be judged based on its originality, emotionally compelling nature and sincerity. See official rules on following page.

Send your entry to:
Mother's Day Contest

In Canada
P.O. Box 637
Fort Erie, Ontario
L2A 5X3

In U.S.A.
P.O. Box 9076
3010 Walden Ave.
Buffalo, NY
14269-9076

Or enter online at www.eHarlequin.com

PRROY

HARLEQUIN MOTHER'S DAY CONTEST 2216
OFFICIAL RULES
NO PURCHASE NECESSARY TO ENTER

Two ways to enter:

• **Via The Internet:** Log on to the Harlequin romance website (www.eHarlequin.com) anytime beginning 12:01 a.m. E.S.T., January 1, 2002 through 11:59 p.m. E.S.T., April 1, 2002 and follow the directions displayed on-line to enter your name, address (including zip code), e-mail address and in 100 words or fewer, describe how your mother helped with the romance in your life.

• **Via Mail:** Handprint (or type) on an 8 1/2" x 11" plain piece of paper, your name, address (including zip code) and e-mail address (if you have one), and in 100 words or fewer, describe how your mother helped with the romance in your life. Mail your entry via first-class mail to: Harlequin Mother's Day Contest 2216, (in the U.S.) P.O. Box 9076, Buffalo, NY 14269-9076; (in Canada) P.O. Box 637, Fort Erie, Ontario, Canada L2A 5X3.

For eligibility, entries must be submitted either through a completed Internet transmission or postmarked no later than 11:59 p.m. E.S.T., April 1, 2002 (mail-in entries must be received by April 9, 2002). Limit one entry per person, household address and e-mail address. On-line and/or mailed entries received from persons residing in geographic areas in which entry is not permissible will be disqualified.

Entries will be judged by a panel of judges, consisting of members of the Harlequin editorial, marketing and public relations staff using the following criteria:
- Originality - 50%
- Emotional Appeal - 25%
- Sincerity - 25%

In the event of a tie, duplicate prizes will be awarded. Decisions of the judges are final.

Prize: A 6-night/7-day stay for two at the Inter-Continental San Juan Resort & Casino, including round-trip coach air transportation from gateway airport nearest winner's home (approximate retail value: $4,000). Prize includes breakfast daily and a mother and daughter day of beauty at the beachfront hotel's spa. Prize consists of only those items listed as part of the prize. Prize is valued in U.S. currency.

All entries become the property of Torstar Corp. and will not be returned. No responsibility is assumed for lost, late, illegible, incomplete, inaccurate, non-delivered or misdirected mail or misdirected e-mail, for technical, hardware or software failures of any kind, lost or unavailable network connections, or failed, incomplete, garbled or delayed computer transmission or any human error which may occur in the receipt or processing of the entries in this Contest.

Contest open only to residents of the U.S. (except Colorado) and Canada, who are 18 years of age or older and is void wherever prohibited by law; all applicable laws and regulations apply. Any litigation within the Province of Quebec respecting the conduct or organization of a publicity contest may be submitted to the Régie des jeux des alcools, des courses et des jeux for a ruling. Any litigation respecting the awarding of a prize may be submitted to the Régie des alcools, des courses et des jeux only for the purpose of helping the parties reach a settlement. Employees and immediate family members of Torstar Corp. and D.L. Blair, Inc., their affiliates, subsidiaries and all other agencies, entities and persons connected with the use, marketing or conduct of this Contest are not eligible to enter. Taxes on prize are the sole responsibility of winner. Acceptance of any prize offered constitutes permission to use winner's name, photograph or other likeness for the purposes of advertising, trade and promotion on behalf of Torstar Corp., its affiliates and subsidiaries without further compensation to the winner, unless prohibited by law.

Winner will be determined no later than April 15, 2002 and be notified by mail. Winner will be required to sign and return an Affidavit of Eligibility form within 15 days after winner notification. Non-compliance within that time period may result in disqualification and an alternate winner may be selected. Wianer of trip must execute a Release of Liability prior to ticketing and must possess required travel documents (e.g. Passport, photo ID) where applicable. Travel must be completed within 12 months of selection and is subject to traveling companion completing and returning a Release of Liability prior to travel; and hotel and flight accommodations availability. Certain restrictions and blackout dates may apply. No substitution of prize permitted by winner. Torstar Corp. and D.L. Blair, Inc., their parents, affiliates, and subsidiaries are not responsible for errors in printing or electronic presentation of Contest, or entries. In the event of printing or other errors which may result in unintended prize values or duplication of prizes, all affected entries shall be null and void. If for any reason the Internet portion of the Contest is not capable of running as planned, including infection by computer virus, bugs, tampering, unauthorized intervention, fraud, technical failures, or any other causes beyond the control of Torstar Corp. which corrupt or affect the administration, secrecy, fairness, integrity or proper conduct of the Contest, Torstar Corp. reserves the right, at its sole discretion, to disqualify any individual who tampers with the entry process and to cancel, terminate, modify or suspend the Contest or the Internet portion thereof. In the event the Internet portion must be terminated a notice will be posted on the website and all entries received prior to termination will be judged in accordance with these rules. In the event of a dispute regarding an on-line entry, the entry will be deemed submitted by the authorized holder of the e-mail account submitted at the time of entry. Authorized account holder is defined as the natural person who is assigned to an e-mail address by an Internet access provider, on-line service provider or other organization that is responsible for arranging e-mail address for the domain associated with the submitted e-mail address. Torstar Corp. and/or D.L. Blair Inc. assumes no responsibility for any computer injury or damage related to or resulting from accessing and/or downloading any sweepstakes material. Rules are subject to any requirements/ limitations imposed by the FCC. Purchase or acceptance of a product offer does not improve your chances of winning.

For winner's name (available after May 1, 2002), send a self-addressed, stamped envelope to: Harlequin Mother's Day Contest Winners 2216, P.O. Box 4200 Blair, NE 68009-4200 or you may access the www.eHarlequin.com Web site through June 3, 2002.

Contest sponsored by Torstar Corp., P.O. Box 9042, Buffalo, NY 14269-9042.